The Savant

of

Chelsea

Suzanne Jenkins

The Savant of Chelsea
by Suzanne Jenkins

For information on the *Greektown* trilogy, the *Pam of Babylon*
series, and other works by author Suzanne Jenkins, please refer
to the 'Also by…' section at the end of this novel.

Author's Note

In 1987, I went on a business trip to New Orleans with my husband, Jim, and fell in love with the city. The only dark place in the trip was my concern for the horses that pulled tourist carriages around the French Quarter. I had an idea for a story that would not go away, about a little girl who was being abused (even that far back it was a theme in my work) who heard the thoughts of the horses. In the story called *Alexandra's Gift*, the abuse caused a sort of mental illness, which led to the gift of communicating with the horses. Unfortunately, once I started writing, it reminded me too much of the old Mr. Ed television series, so I abandoned the work for a while. But Alexandra stuck in my head. Writing her story became a therapeutic vehicle for me to write of my own experiences as a sexual abuse survivor. I spent several years writing about it and, fortunately for the reader, deleted all but a short chapter in the current manuscript.

Alexandra morphed from a child into an adult in the early nineties when I read about Kathleen Durst, who went missing in 1982. Her story was compelling enough, but when I read about her husband, Robert Alan, I was hooked. He'd witnessed his mother's suicide when he was seven, and doctors believed the experience led to a diagnosis of schizophrenia. There are a string of disappearances among his female acquaintances which have never been solved. Alexandra's personality was developing as I read more about the aftermath of trauma in children.

Next, I became obsessed with the notion that exercise could help individuals with Tourette's syndrome have more control over their symptoms. I met a young man in 1994 with Tourette's syndrome when I used to race through the Jersey Pine Barrens with the South Jersey Outdoor Club on their Friday night runs. I brought up the rear as we did fifteen miles in the moonlight. He said the consistent, sustained exercise helped him keep his symptoms under control. Alexandra is an obsessive exerciser, which allows her to function in the role her genius affords her.

Over the past twenty-five years, Alexandra has developed from a grotesque monster into an attractive woman who ends up with an entire community behind her. The reader is not going to know what happens after the climax; it is up to you to decide. Needless to say, this is a work that I'm sure will have a division between those who hate my writing and those who love it.

I'm trying to write something lighthearted, but it's just not my forte.

Thank you so much for your support and your reviews. I love readers, and since I love storytelling, I hope you'll be entertained at the very least.

Chapter 1

Surgical services are often hidden away at the core of a hospital. Isolated from the rest of the facility, OR staff members work in anonymity. They come into the building dressed in street clothes, unlike the other employees who are uniformed, changing into garb that covers all their identifiable parts, including their sexuality in some instances. Hair is covered with a hat, face with a mask, and everyone wears the same color scrubs.

Alexandra Donicka fit the example to a tee. She appeared asexual. Very tall for a woman, painfully thin from continuously running long distance, she didn't wear makeup, so you couldn't tell by looking at her eyes. New employees or sales reps who had access to a room while a case was underway often didn't know until she pulled her sterile gown off that Dr. Donicka was a woman. She had small breasts and didn't wear a bra; they took on a life of their own if she was hurrying along. While running, they were positively animated, often bouncing in opposite directions. She was oblivious to it, and to the commotion her breasts caused.

"I can't stand her." It was not an unusual proclamation by the nursing staff and others who had to work closely with Alexandra. Many of the anesthesia staff felt the same way.

"If I had to work with her every day, I'd quit," a young nurse said. "I don't know how Grace does it."

"How Grace does what?" Grace Hendrix walked into the staff lounge for coffee while her room was being cleaned between cases.

"How you work with Donicka. She makes my skin crawl," the nurse replied.

"She's okay," Jeff Albertson said. He was a nurse anesthetist assigned to the neurosurgical service. "My problem with her is that she's nuts."

"Stop," Grace said. "She's fine."

"She's nuts," Jeff replied. "Certifiable."

"Shush, here she comes," another nurse said. Everyone turned back to their coffee or newspapers or iPhones as Alexandra pushed the door to the lounge open. She walked over to Grace and stood next to her, silently.

"Would you like a graham cracker?" Grace asked.

She nodded her head.

Grace opened the package and gave it to her, like offering a toddler a snack.

"I'll order your lunch now," Grace said, looking over at Jeff. "Is that okay with you?" The next patient was in the holding area, and as soon as the room was clean, they'd prepare to bring him in for his surgery, a tumor dissection that often held surprises. It was a good thing the surgeon was going to eat now. She might not get another chance for hours.

"I guess so. Randy already interviewed the patient, so as soon as the room is ready, we can get started." Jeff actually hated it that the surgeon du jour was pampered, her food ordered, the schedule possibly held up so she could have her meal. Her partner, Eb Whitmore, had the reputation of being a prick, but at least he wasn't a prima donna. Randy, the senior resident, would take over the duties of positioning the patient on the OR table, and everything would be ready by the time she was done eating.

Randy was counting the days until he could flee from this hellhole on the banks of the East River, and retreat to a clean, wealthy community hospital in Princeton. In the meantime, he realized what a tremendous opportunity it had been for him to work with Alexandra Donicka; the mention of her name on his résumé had guaranteed a lucrative partnership with a growing practice in his hometown. He could be civil for six more months.

After housekeeping finished cleaning the room, the team of nurses who worked with Alexandra got busy setting up for the next case. Large, stainless-steel tables covered with sterile drapes would hold the instruments needed for the surgery. Virginia, the operating room technician, scrubbed in to set up the case and assist Alexandra. She'd worked with Alexandra since the day she arrived as a resident and was able to anticipate the surgeon's every move after all these years. The other nurses and techs were amazed that she could tolerate the surgeon and even happier they didn't have to work with her.

"She's easy," Virginia said, defending Alexandra. "She never talks, never yells, never changes her routine. I can sit on a stool and daydream all day if I want. I'm sixty-five years old; this is my last gig. I'll take it."

Grace poured Alexandra a glass of orange juice as she called into Room 11, the OR suite where neurosurgical cases were done. Jeff answered the phone. "You can tell Randy to take the patient into the room," she said. Randy had been assisting on her cases since he started his residency in neurosurgery. Soon, it would fall to someone else, but for now, he was the lucky one.

The case proceeded without incident. Alexandra did one difficult case after another, bent over the operating table, speechless, reaching for her own instruments, rarely looking up. By late afternoon, the small of her back was starting to complain, a little niggling pain that bore into her and crept down her legs. She stood up straight, stretching a little bit. Then she went back to work. When the final case was over, she asked Randy if he'd see the patient to the recovery room. It wasn't standard practice for the surgeon to leave the room until the patient was off the table, but it was another special bending of the rules done for Dr. Donicka.

∽∾

She made it through the day, avoiding as many encounters as she could without seeming rude, and at the end of it, simply no longer caring. She had to get out of there. The locker room was empty when she reached it. Opening her locker, she dug out the same running clothes she had come to work in, still damp with sweat. Her assistant had packed clean clothes for her, placing them neatly in a pile on the shelf, but she ignored them. All she cared about was getting on the pavement. Taking the back staircase to avoid running into anyone in the hall, other surgeons or members of the hospital board needing her opinion, all the while she in her smelly running clothes, trying to squelch a scream.

The packed hospital lobby teemed with visitors. Standing off to the side out of the way, hospital administrator Peter Van Sant was chatting with board members when his eye caught disheveled Alexandra coming out of the stairwell. The others in the group followed his eyes and didn't miss the vision of their prize surgeon striding through the crowds, using her elbows if needed to push the unwary out of the way.

"Oh my," Nelda Smith said, shaking her head. "Some things never change."

"She did almost six hundred surgeries last year," Van Sant replied defensively.

Nelda shook her head. "I thought she'd grow out of it by now, or at least adapt."

"We knew she was sick when we begged her to sign on," Peter said. "I don't care what she looks like or how she acts. She's the best neurosurgeon in the country." It was true; other doctors sent their patients to the Medical Center for a consultation with the famed, albeit kooky Alexandra Donicka. Peter Van Sant thought it was a stroke of luck they'd discovered her while she was in medical school. A professor at Columbia, someone Peter had known for years, contacted him before Match Day.

"I've got someone here you should consider, Pete," Don Bender said. "She's got a few mental issues, but with support she'd do fine."

"Why the hell would I consider someone with mental issues?" Peter asked.

"Trust me," Don replied. "This woman is brilliant. That doesn't even cover it. She's a genius." She also had a sixth sense that wasn't part of her résumé, but it was known among her superiors, something that definitely made her few eccentricities worth dealing with.

"Be more specific. Is she schizophrenic? Bipolar?" Peter was getting interested now.

"No, she has a personality disorder," he answered. "It's sort of a tick, but she controls it by exercise," he said, minimizing her problems.

Over the years, Don had never made a recommendation that didn't work out, so Peter decided to take a chance. He and Eb Whitmore, the head of the neurosurgical department, made an appointment to interview Alexandra before Match Day. They took a cab across town to meet her. The first impression was not good. Her appearance was startling enough; she was almost six feet tall and couldn't weigh much more than one hundred pounds. Her hair was unwieldy; bright orange, curly and uncombed, it stood out from her head like a giant afro. But when she looked up at Peter, he was taken aback; she was beautiful. She had huge, brown eyes and clear skin, not a freckle on her face. Rarely making eye contact, her gaze was penetrating when she did. Peter decided she had more than a few mental issues after trying to talk to her. Her gifts had better be outstanding or she would be left for some other institution to grab up.

In most cases, interviews were with the student alone. But in Alexandra's case, she had a student shadow and her advisor tag along. They provided Peter with stacks of recommendations that included explanations why her assets far outweighed the extra considerations that would be necessary.

"Can you answer questions?" Peter asked her directly.

"As long as they're scientific," Alexandra answered bluntly.

He tried to hide a grin. *Add bitch to her résumé*, he thought. She didn't say, but it would soon be evident that she was unable or unwilling to discuss anything of a personal nature, incapable of self-praise. Years later, Eb Whitmore said it was eerily as though she didn't *know* how good she was. She didn't blow her own horn because she couldn't.

They made the decision on the spot to offer Alexandra a residency with NYMC before any other facility found out about her, and it would include a full-time, personal assistant.

They discovered this would be necessary after the fact because she was also incapable of taking care of herself: bathing, dressing appropriately, eating and getting anywhere on time. Peter Van Sant hoped he hadn't made a very big and very expensive mistake.

❦

Unaware of the observers, Alexandra pushed through the crowded lobby, gasping for breath as she went through the huge glass doors to the outside. She took two steps at a time, her goal to get to the sidewalk as fast as she could. Her tiredness from the workday forgotten, she was invigorated by the bright sunlight and cool air. She ran down First Avenue from Midtown to Delancey, through Chinatown and over to Battery Park. She ran back and forth, across town from the East River to the Hudson River. She'd walk back to Eighth in Chelsea, stopping at the local bodega across the street from her apartment for a cup of coffee. It was all she had an appetite for, and she liked it strong and black.

She *was* exhausted from running. Unlocking the door to her building using a key on a string around her neck, she slowly climbed up the stairs to the second floor. Her assistant left a sandwich and fruit for her on the kitchen counter, with a list itemizing her evening routine. She picked it up and took it into her bedroom with the coffee. At the windowsill was a tall wooden stool, and she'd sit there and eat while watching the last of rush-hour traffic inch along Eighth Avenue.

A light, freezing rain had begun to fall, giving the evening a sparkly, mirrored look. The red brake lights of the cars and green neon sign of the coffee shop across the street reminded her of Christmas. That was all the season would be; decorated public places, the plain and boring transformed into the magical for a few short weeks. Soon, it really would be Christmas. There would be no tree here in this tiny apartment, or gifts. There was no need. She sat in the dark apartment, looking out the window for hours. Her sweaty clothes dried and stiffened on her body. Following the directions on her routine list, she remembered to refill her water glass repeatedly as the evening turned into night.

At midnight, her watch beeped. She got up and stretched, reluctant to end the reverie at the window. If it had been the weekend, she'd stay there all night, watching. Her neighbors directly across the street kept their shades drawn closed, knowing from experience that she would be there, looking out at the street.

She stripped naked and turned the water on in the shower stall. Not waiting for it to warm up, she stepped under the freezing cold shower. She hated bathing. It had nothing to do with wanting to be dirty or fearing cleanliness. Washing her body meant touching herself. Her flat, skeletal frame felt awful under her hands. She bathed now because it was part of her routine, in case she had to go out in the night to answer an emergency call from the hospital. If it happened, Randy would call her, and then the hospital operator would call a car to pick her up. She'd been caught running to work in the middle of the night when someone saw her come in covered in sweat with her running clothes on. That mistake wouldn't be made again. It was too dangerous, and she was too valuable to the hospital.

She pulled on sweat pants and a T-shirt and got into bed.

Chapter 2

The recurring dream was an episode from her childhood that she unconsciously revisited from time to time. She was ten years old, on the streets of New Orleans alone, after dark. A small, black dog was chasing her block after block, biting her ankles and hanging on to the back of her dress with his pointed teeth. In the dream, as it had been in reality, she ran to her house, the shack she shared with her mother at the back of a brick courtyard. But when she attempted to push open the door, it was locked. The little girl screamed the rarely spoken name, "Mommy, Mommy! Open the door." All the while the dog tugged at her clothes. She swatted at him, screaming, "Please go away. Leave me alone!" Then she heard the same words coming from within the shack. "Go away. Leave me alone!"

In her dream, she spent eternity at the mercy of the small, black dog. In reality, a stranger came to her rescue and batted the dog away with his cane. The little girl staggered to a neighbor's porch, the house dark and quiet. Climbing the stairs, she didn't feel fear, just exhaustion and cold. She hid behind a white wicker settee, waiting, hoping her mother would unlock the door for her. She finally fell asleep. The turquoise light of sunrise was visible between the buildings of Jackson Square when the door to the shack opened, waking her up as a man in a riding costume walked out. She could hear her mother's voice, cheerful and sweet, but couldn't see her. The man walked across the courtyard, and the child saw that what he was wearing was the uniform of the mounted police.

His horse wasn't there, but he had the jodhpurs on, and there was a belt with a gun in a holster hanging from it buckled around his waist. He had taken the time to dress with care while the child froze in the outdoors.

When he was out of sight and earshot, her mother reopened the door and, snarling, whispered, "Alexandra, get in here."

Alexandra crept out from behind the settee and, with resolution and courage, went down the porch stairs and across the cobblestones, knowing what was waiting for her when the door closed again.

కావ

The adult Alexandra didn't acknowledge the dream. It woke her at the correct time in the morning. She would go through the motions of her daily life without thought, with the direction she got from the people around her. A glass of water, poured by her assistant the previous day, sat at the bedside. Pulling the covers from her legs, she swung them out over the side of the bed, stood up, and walked over to the uncurtained window. Still dark out, she examined the buildings across the street for other lights but saw none. Looking to her right, toward the East River, there wasn't light yet from the sun. The ever-present fog—eerily moving down the street, white, luminescent fingers gyrating and curling along, and reaching out for the pavement—invited her to join it. She drained the glass of water and pulled on running clothes again. The same routine, day after day, made it possible for her to fulfill her obligations at work and still have the time she needed for the important run. Without it, there was no functioning in society.

Her feet struck the pavement lightly, but with enough force that the energy traveled up her slender legs, settling in her lower back. She'd feel it later in the day, when standing for hours at the surgical field taxed her skeleton in the extreme. Due to the exercise, she was barely able to maintain her weight.

When she returned home two hours later, there was a black limousine parked in front of her apartment. She could see her assistant, Loren, standing in the bedroom window, looking down at her, shaking her head. Alexandra bounded up the stairs, hard-earned restraint keeping her from taking off again down Eighth Avenue.

"You're late," Loren singsonged, standing at the top of the stairs. "James has a bag and your briefcase. Go on ahead. You can shower at the hospital." She handed Alexandra a juice box and a granola bar, like a child. With a waving motion, but not daring to touch her, she pointed back down the stairs. "Go on now."

"I could've run to work," Alexandra argued.

"Tomorrow," said Loren.

Her driver, James was waiting with the limo door opened. He nodded his head, acknowledging her, but didn't greet her. She wouldn't have responded anyway. Grace would be waiting at the entrance to the hospital, anxious to get Alexandra ready for work.

On her operating room days, she was expected to be there at six thirty in the morning. Today's schedule was busy, one neurosurgical case after another. She worked like a robot, with little feeling about what she did all day. She figured she must be good at it; those around her told her enough times. It was automatic. Her job was to view films, operate, and nothing more. The hospital hierarchy had her on a short leash. She was shielded from awake patients and visitors as much as possible.

Or, they were shielded from her. Senior residents were her eyes and ears. Her reputation for surgical excellence was known around the world, but the staff tried to hide her *eccentricity* when it was possible.

The driver glanced in the rearview mirror. Alexandra's face, pressed to the window, looked pathetic. He couldn't believe that she was able to live independently, let alone practice medicine. The limo slid into place at the front entrance of the hospital. Grace was waiting, dressed in a green surgeon's gown. Alexandra didn't wait for James to open the limo door for her, hopping out and ignoring Grace, who followed her into the hospital with a briefcase and the bag containing clean underwear and clothes to go home in. In the elevator, Grace spoke.

"Long run this morning," she stated as a fact.

Alexandra nodded her head. But she continued to nod, seemingly unable to quit. Slowly raising her hand, the nurse gently placed her fingertips on the back of Alexandra's head. The forbidden touch jolted the surgeon out of her movement. *Obviously not long enough,* Grace thought. It was not a good sign. Exercise was the method by which Alexandra's tics and spasms were controlled. Grace hoped the effort of a grueling operating schedule would be enough. In the meantime, she would push her to shower and change into scrubs and try to make up for the minutes that were ticking by faster and faster, making her late and, worse, falling behind.

Alexandra was oblivious to her day, never faltering in her responsibilities. Like a machine able to stand at the side of an OR table, hunched over the patient for hours at a time, she never complained. But she did have her limits. Something about the way she was treated at work that day reminded her of an incident in her childhood. She abhorred any memories that might flit through her head, but this one stuck fast that day.

She was only seven years old. Her mother hadn't come home for over a week. Julia, Alexandra's neighbor, wasn't aware of the atrocity taking place in her own backyard. Every day that week, Alexandra got up in the morning, dressed in the same clothes she had been wearing for days, brushed her teeth, and ate whatever she could find in the house to eat. She happily skipped to school. In the afternoon, she'd return to an empty house. Playing alone in the courtyard was her favorite activity anyway. It was peaceful with her mother gone.

By Wednesday, her teacher was suspicious that the child was still wearing the same dress and had a dirty face. She was never clean, but this was getting ridiculous. Miss Adams was her name, Alexandra remembered much later. Miss Adams went down to the nurse's office with the little girl in tow and left her there. The nurse gently took Alexandra by the hand and led her to the sink. She picked her up and sat her on the counter. Holding her hand, she used her free hand to squeeze soap through a small terry cloth towel. It was white and soft. The memory of the cloth stayed with Alexandra for years. The warmth of it, the way the nurse gently wiped Alexandra's face and hands clean, and then dried it with another soft, white cloth, was one of the few acts of kindness she experienced. The memory of the beating she got when the school tracked down her mother and admonished her for abandoning the child would vanish soon after.

Alexandra didn't feel physical pain. She had little sense of her physical body. She didn't see dirt on her face or feel hunger, didn't notice if her clothes were on backwards or upside down. Many of the negative things she experienced failed to move her. She went through the motions of living as any child did, enjoying her little friends, craving the attention of the adults who were in her life, and performing for them in whatever way they seemed to require. The teachers got tremendous results for minimal effort; her mother got perfect behavior and obedience. Her life was one of few surprises and joyful moments. She shook her head, trying to rid her mind of these thoughts. *What good does it do?*

She got through another OR schedule and left the hospital the same way she did the previous day—with one goal and that was to get out of there and run until she was ready to drop.

∂∘⊷

At five the next morning, after another restless, dream-filled night, the telephone rang. Alexandra woke up right away and reached over for it. She thought it was the hospital. But it was her old neighbor Julia. Alexandra sat up in bed.

"Julia," she said, not used to talking to her this early.

"Alex, are you awake? I woke you, didn't I? Forgive me, dear, will you?" She gave her a few seconds to respond, and when she didn't, as expected, Julia continued. Her voice was soothing. She had a slight southern twang, although she wasn't originally from New Orleans. Living there for as long as she had and rarely returning back east had its effect.

"Well, I hardly know where to begin. So I'll just get it out, dear. Your momma died. Yes, she died. It seems so unlikely, she was so young, but there you go. Let me know if you understand what I'm telling you, Alexandra," Julia asked, waiting for an answer. She could hear a slight murmur on the other end of the line.

"Dube called me at midnight. He was in a tizzy, Alexandra. You know how he used to get? I couldn't understand a word he was saying, and finally, one of his daughters got on the phone, the fat one, the funny one. You remember her name, don't you?"

"Tess," Alexandra whispered.

"Tess, of course, Tess. She took the phone from Dube and told me that your momma took to her bed yesterday afternoon, wouldn't come down for the dinner crowd. Evidently, Dube was as mad as a rabid dog, sent one of the other waitresses up to her room, and she found her. She did it herself. There is no reason for me to lie to you, my dear, none at all. The truth is what you need, all of it, no matter how painful. The truth. Now maybe we can get the truth about the *other matter*. Are you there, honey? I am so sorry about this, but there was no other way to tell you. I knew you would want to act as fast as you can." Julia stopped. She knew from experience that a dead line didn't necessarily mean there was no one there. She waited for a few moments, and finally, Alexandra spoke.

"I heard you, Julia."

"Dear, what do you want me to do?" Julia asked.

"I'll have to make some calls here to, you know, cover me, but I want to think for a while about what I have to do." The truth was she was flabbergasted because just yesterday she had to remind herself that there was purpose to her life, to what she was willing to sacrifice. And it had come to this overnight. Now she had to act quickly, while there were high emotions all around. She would manipulate those who had been close to her mother. She had to gather information while they were still in the state of grief.

She said, "I have to find out who might know something about where *baby Elizabeth* is."

15

Julia didn't respond. She was stunned that Alexandra would mention the baby already.

"Julia, thank you for calling me. I'll call you later, if that's okay," Alexandra said.

"Yes, of course, do what you need to do. I'll be in and out all morning, but you can leave a message, okay? I'll talk to you soon?"

"Yes, soon. Good-bye, Julia." Alexandra didn't wait for a response. She was thinking, thinking. The key was to move quickly. But it was still too early in the day to do anything, so she would go out to run. It would clear her head, help her think. Her nerves were raw. Skin tingling, she pulled on her running clothes, grabbed her key, put it around her neck, and went out the door into the cold and foggy dawn.

Chapter 3

Her mother. When was the last time she thought of her mother? What she thought of was her mother's acts, but not the actual woman. *She is dead. She took her own life. It's better that she's dead. She was insane, miserable. She's better off dead,* she thought repeatedly. Each strike of the pavement increased the sense of purpose Alexandra had. There was so much to do, but she could only take one step at a time. She turned around after running uptown and started going south, toward home. She would be late, again. When she let herself into the apartment, it was almost seven. James was in the car out in front while Loren was pacing in the kitchen. Alexandra walked through the kitchen, head down, knowing she had displeased everyone once again.

"Sorry," she said, the first time she'd apologized for making them wait. Then she remembered her mother had died. She would use it to get back into their favor. She focused her eyes on Loren, the first time in years she'd made eye contact with her. "My mother died yesterday."

Loren dropped her hands and rushed over to Alexandra, but stopped before she invaded her space.

"I'm so sorry! Do you want me to call the hospital for you?" she said, truly concerned.

"No, I'm going in today," she said softly, resigned. She walked into her bedroom and stood looking out the window, suddenly tired. She wanted to crawl back into bed. She saw James in the long, black car, the hood wet with a light falling rain, exhaust visible in the early morning light. She felt incapable of making a move.

Loren saw the hesitation. "Your clothes are in the car. Why not run on to work, and I'll have James meet you there?"

Alexandra sprang to life without saying a word. She dashed out of the apartment, down the steps to the front door. James got out to open the limo door for her and shook his head when she ignored him and started running toward the hospital.

After Loren sent James to the hospital, she stepped back into the apartment to call the OR and tell Grace Alexandra's mother died yesterday. *Who even knew she had a living mother?* Grace would call the neuroscience division and tell May, Alexandra's office assistant.

∽∾

By the time Alexandra got to the hospital, showered and dressed, the waiting room of her office was packed. She entered through a separate door, isolated from the patients. May went to her as soon as she arrived.

"What can I do for you?" she asked.

Alexandra hesitated. Her eyes switched back and forth from May's neck to the floor. She was struggling to speak. May gently placed her hand on the doctor's back and pushed her toward the lounge. She repeated, "What can I do for you, Doctor?"

Alexandra said, "Get me a ticket for New Orleans Saturday morning."

"Okay, I can do that," May answered. "Anything else?"

Alexandra didn't respond, so May continued, hoping they'd be able to catch up.

"Randy's seeing patients with you. He's in with your first one now. Here are her films." She moved over to the viewing box, stuck the first from a pile of MRI films up onto the screen, and switched the light on. May left the room, knowing that any attempt at conversation was futile when films were up. Once that happened, Alexandra wasn't aware of anything but the negative imagery lit up before her. The white, grays and black of the film took over. What was invisible to most eyes was revealed to hers. The slightest curve, divot, change of shadow, outlined structure and abnormality stood out. With her eyes focused on film, she was able to speak in a normal tone, with confidence, interested. The staff used it as the only time she spoke to the patient and their family. Alexandra knew she must measure her words when there was a possibility of a horrific diagnosis. She also knew that patients weren't given a final diagnosis until after surgery, if surgery was needed, or after many tests were run.

Randy came out to get her. "Ready, Doctor? Your next patient is a sixteen-year-old female with a rapid onset of grand mal seizures two months ago." He kept up a steady stream of facts regarding the drugs tried to control the seizures, waiting for some information about the film.

She finally spoke, so quietly that he had to lean close to her to hear. "There's nothing I can see. Let's do another EEG today."

They came to the door of the examination room, and Randy opened it for her like a gentleman, allowing her to go through first. He introduced her to the young woman and her parents, watching closely to see if she was appropriately responding. She smiled at them without opening her mouth as though to scream. She walked over to the viewing box in the room while Randy explained that she would show them the MRI. Alexandra spoke quietly. She explained they needed to do another EEG. They would be guided by it and make any decisions about treatment then. She lowered her head and walked out of the room, back to the viewing desk. This scenario would repeat itself throughout the day, different patients with different symptoms and different diagnoses. Randy did most of the dirty work, breaking the news to patients whose MRIs showed obvious tumors.

Finally, blessedly, office hours were finished. Her daily response was repeated: get out of work clothes, pull on her sweaty clothes from the morning, and run as fast as she could out of the building onto the streets. She felt as though she would explode if she spent one more second there. She pushed through the hallways crowded with secretaries and medical assistants. If they didn't move quickly, she'd run them down. They'd press themselves up against the hallway walls, making room for her. Not everyone cared that she was a surgeon, and occasionally someone would yell, "Watch it!" or refuse to move. She didn't even notice and would just barrel right through.

It had been a particularly nerve-racking day because she needed to think. She needed to be free of anything that would get in her way of planning her next move. Her mother's death was monumental. It was something she had been waiting for; something that she needed, but didn't think would come about so soon.

With each step, she felt her body relax, her mind slow down. The pressure in her back disappeared; the tension in her face was gone. Her long legs covered the miles without effort.

Her mind was blank except for planning. Planning would be purposeful, intentional. She didn't understand epiphany. Once she finished this run, she would call Julia back. Tonight she would decide what her plan would be once she got back to New Orleans. The pretense was she was going for a funeral. Nothing could have been further from the truth.

Chapter 4

The past week had been hell for George Dube. On Friday, his mistress of over forty years, Miss Catherine Donicka, didn't come downstairs to start her shift as a waitress at his restaurant, The Black Swan. He sent another waitress, Jemma, to see what was keeping her. The young woman came screaming down the stairs in tears, yelling, "She's dead!" for the whole house to hear.

He did his best to shut her up, going up the steep flight of stairs as fast as his three-hundred-pound body could go. Catherine's room was at the end of the hall. He reached it with a crowd of his employees at his heels. He growled, "Get back downstairs." Dube waited until they turned around, looking over their shoulders. He was afraid to go into the room. She wasn't lying on her bed or at the desk, or on the floor, so the bathroom was the only place left.

She was on the floor, surrounded by blood all over the white tile and her body, both wrists slashed. The bathroom was small; it was hard for Dube to maneuver around, and he struggled when he tried to crouch down to see if he could feel a pulse in her neck. There wasn't one. All he could think of was the police storming up the stairway that came down into the dining room as the dinner crowd was just coming in. Once he was able to straighten up, he backed out of the tiny room into her bedroom and stood there for a moment, thinking. Shoe prints of congealed blood followed him. Tess, his oldest daughter, came into the room.

"What happened, Papa? Jemma said Catherine's dead," she said.

He looked at her and nodded. Since he didn't acknowledge Alexandra as his child, he thought Tess was the smartest and had a good sense of the restaurant business. He'd ignored her; she'd been after him for years to get Catherine help. He'd been responsible for her all her life, doing the best he could to take care of her, and now it was over. Dube felt tremendous relief. Recently, she'd taken to wandering around the French Quarter, talking to herself and shouting at people. He gave her only one or two tables a night to wait on, more than she could handle. It never occurred to him to let her retire. Her mental status had deteriorated. *Now, what to tell the police? If only he had come up to look for her himself. Then, she could've lain there until closing. No one would have known, he'd have said she was unwell.* Now, Tess was here, he would let her handle it; it was really more than he could bear.

Tess took him by the hand and led him out of the horror scene, down to his own room. The telephone was in the hall. She phoned the police, telling them to come to the rear of the restaurant, and she would meet them in the alley. Behind the kitchen was a little-used stairway that went up to the third floor used for servants in the old days. They would have to use it. She had a business to run, and they weren't going to traipse through the dining room, upsetting everyone.

Tess was furious she had to deal with the mess. Catherine had been an embarrassment to the family for as long as she could remember. Her father was mush in the woman's hands.

The strange thing was he always insisted that she work even when she was really too ill to wait tables. His wife, Emma, had lived a *rich man's wife's* life, playing bridge, shopping, going to Europe on buying trips for a shop she ran with her mother. She wasn't one to poke around in his business, so he got away with a lot. She ignored his infidelities. Tess tried to reason with her mother, encourage her to divorce Dube, but she wouldn't discuss it. She loved her life, had all the money and freedom she could ask for, lovely daughters, and great friends.

When Dube banished Catherine and Alexandra to the chicken coop, it was a mixed blessing. The family was relieved that she was out of the house, but worried because of the child. Emma forbad anyone to help Catherine after they left. Tess was heartbroken. She was a year older than Alexandra was, and they had been fast friends. They ate together, slept together, planned on going to school together. Then, overnight, she was gone. For months, Tess cried herself to sleep every night. Now, the adult Tess, in the privacy of her room, cried for what was gone, what would never be. Because she knew Catherine was her real mother, too, she would allow herself this one night of anguish, and then she would move on, as she had trained herself to do from the age of five.

Chapter 5

The child Alexandra loved her new home and neighborhood away from the restaurant. It was a familiar sight to see the little redheaded girl running and playing. She knew not to venture anywhere near The Black Swan now that she no longer lived there. When she got hungry, she would go back to the little house and eat fruit or bread; it wasn't for another year or so that she got the hang of the can opener and figured out how to turn the stove on and off.

The house was a refurbished chicken coop situated at the back of a courtyard reached by going through a brick paved alleyway, under an arched doorway, which was covered with ivy. At the front of the courtyard was a brick building that housed the museum Julia ran. Dube owned the building and rented it out to the City of New Orleans Historical Foundation. Every morning at ten, she'd meet a group of tourists in the courtyard in front of Alexandra's house and tell them about all the important people who had visited the museum over the years. She lowered her voice in case Catherine was sleeping. Alexandra loved it when the people would be crowded around the courtyard.

The house was one big room with an attic. The furniture was leftover cast-offs from Dube: a big couch that turned into a bed for Catherine, a small table with two chairs, and a ladder that led to the attic. In one corner a makeshift kitchen was set up with a sink, a small icebox and a two-burner hot plate. To reach the bathroom, you had to go out a door in the back of the house to an enclosed brick paved courtyard and into a shed that Dube had built. Alexandra's bedroom was in the attic. She had a cot and a box to hold her clothes. There was a cubbyhole in the wall where she hid when she was alone. One night, Catherine made a rare visit up the ladder after work and got angry when she couldn't find Alexandra. After that, Alexandra was careful to come out of the cubbyhole and get into her cot when she heard her mother return.

Alexandra loved the French Market. When they lived at the restaurant, she would go with Dube or one of the cooks to buy fresh produce and meat for the kitchen. Once they moved, however, the shopping trips stopped. Early on Saturday or Sunday morning, if Catherine didn't come home from work, Alexandra would go alone to watch the pigeons and just hang around. She became a familiar face.

She loved the horse-drawn carriages that took tourists around the Quarter. The horse stables next to the French Market were a block-long row of doors painted green. Every other door led to small apartments where the stable hands lived. The men would often let Alexandra help groom the horses. She was comfortable around the men, and they didn't mind the little girl. They gave her money for her work that she carefully hid from Catherine.

Alexandra loved the narrow streets and little alleyways of the city. At night, she would hide in doorways, watching the tourists. She stayed out of sight in case someone who knew

Catherine went back to The Black Swan to tell her Alexandra was out after dark. She kept an eye out for the police, as well.

At age eight, she was self-sufficient, keeping the little house clean, politely asking her mother for money to buy groceries and cooking her own meals. She excelled at school. Ridiculed because she smelled, she observed her classmates and learned the basics about hygiene and the appropriate clothing for school. She washed and ironed her few dresses, washed her body and brushed her teeth every day. She rarely went to the restaurant unless specifically summoned there by her mother.

Alexandra gave her mother a wide berth, kept quiet when Catherine was home, didn't ask much of her, and didn't give her any reason to notice her. Catherine never saw a report card, never went to a parent conference, and didn't take her daughter to the doctor or dentist. She provided a minimum of security in the form of the chicken coop for her child to live in, and no guidance or protection. Julia was the only adult in Alexandra's life who was available to her in case of a problem, but Alexandra didn't bother her. Alexandra became a master of deceit; she wouldn't complain because there was no one to listen anyway, so she denied herself the luxury of even having fear. Fortunately, she never got a toothache, had minor colds that went away without medication, and no broken arms or bloody noses.

She went to school every day, came home to an empty house every night, and stayed alone until and if her mother came home at two in the morning after the restaurant closed. The weekends continued to be spent staying busy cleaning and doing homework until Catherine left for work. Then she'd go to the French Market to help at the stables. When school was out for the summer, she could go every morning before her mother woke up. She'd quietly get dressed and sneak down the ladder, go out the door, and run to the stables.

༅

Frederick Benson, a new stable hand in New Orleans, watched Alexandra for a few weeks as she brushed and petted the horses, poised and fearless, but obviously lonely and alone. She was a beautiful child, tall with red, curly hair that refused to be captured by barrette or rubber bands, but fine, so it flew around her head like a halo. Frederick Benson liked the way she moved and knew he would attempt to have her before the summer was up. Gaining her trust would be dependent on how well the first encounter went. He decided to let her initiate a meeting. Since his room was right next to the stables, all he did was lead out a horse to groom and she came right over to him. She walked up with a big smile, no fear at all, and began asking questions, offering to help brush the horse he was attending.

It took several days of this voyeurism, Frederick Benson watching her as he groomed his bait, waiting, careful not to make too much of a distraction on the street. By the fourth day, he sat inside his room with the stable door opened, no horse outside on the street, and like clockwork, she appeared. She didn't hesitate to cross his threshold. She was the neediest child he'd ever met. He offered to get her a drink, and she said yes. He ran across the alleyway to a juice stand, Alexandra pleased with the attention shown her.

By the fifth day, he had her dress off; by the sixth, her underpants. She wasn't sexually developed, but welcomed every embrace, looking forward to the abuse. She willingly fulfilled his every request, at times even initiating it. When the time came for intercourse, she didn't refuse him. Frederick

Benson was frightened; he wondered about the parent who was raising her. He grew more cautious, never seeking her out, making sure she wasn't observed by the other stable hands, that she was home before dark, and even bathed her in case the mother got close enough to smell her daughter.

When school started again in the fall, his role became supportive and even protective of the little girl. He'd discovered she had a busybody neighbor who would surely notice if the child didn't show up right after school. He told her to be careful about visiting him. He told her their relationship had to be kept secret because it was illegal and he would go to jail if anyone found out. When she came to him each afternoon, it was always with schoolbooks in hand. She hungered after the attention. She was starting to develop. One day, she came in tears, telling him she had bloodied her panties, and Frederick Benson took over the duties of teaching the young girl about menstruation. He went to the Rexall drug store and bought pads and belts, and the relationship grew in perversity.

She's menstruating; he's fucking her on a nightly basis. What steps should he have taken next? Alexandra got pregnant right away. He didn't think to ask her if her next period came, didn't notice that she seemed paler than usual; no one questioned her lack of appetite because no one cared. Suddenly, one morning five or six months later, it hit him. She was standing in front of him naked, and he noticed her belly—hard, protuberant, and veiny—and her nipples. He had been married once years before, and he remembered the reason for those darkened nipples, and a cold sweat broke out over his skin. Quickly gathering up her clothes, he pushed her into the closet and told her to get dressed. She did so without questioning, and when he told her she'd better get home, she was disappointed.

The next evening when Alexandra returned to the stable and knocked on the door of her molester's room, no one was there. She gently pushed the door, and it opened easily. She entered an empty room, all the belongings of her molester gone. She knew he was gone for good. The pregnant ten-year-old walked the few blocks back home, confused and scared. She didn't know she was pregnant, but the idea she was alone again made her very sad. When she got home, she climbed up the ladder to the attic and, on hands and knees, went into her cubbyhole, and fell asleep.

Chapter 6

The day after Catherine Donicka committed suicide, Dube stayed up in his room for the first time in the memory of the old-timers at The Black Swan Café. Her body was removed and an autopsy done, the mess in the bathroom cleaned up, and business went on as usual. Tess took a tray up to her father's room and sat with him, encouraging him to eat a little dinner. For a man as decisive as Dube, this was strange behavior. Tess told him they needed to contact Alexandra, but she had no idea where she was. Dube said he'd take care of it, he knew where she was and who kept in touch with her. After his daughter left him, the old man picked up the phone and called Julia, who was surprised.

"*Well*, Mr. Dube, to what do I owe the pleasure? You are about the last person I thought I'd hear from," Julia said.

"Save it, chicky. I got problems with you' little doc frien'," he said with a thick accent.

"If you mean Alexandra, I hardly think you could have a problem with her, my dear man. She hasn't been around here for ages," Julia answered, not trying to hide her sarcasm.

"Her momma slashe' her goddamn wrists in my establishment, smart ass," Dube yelled.

"Oh! Well, is she going to be okay?" Julia asked.

"Hell no, she ain't gonna be okay. She dead!" he yelled into the phone.

"Oh, Lord. I beg your pardon, sir. I am truly sorry. I suppose you want me to convey the news," Julia replied.

"Just tell her, will you, please? I got enough troubles here. I let you know what I'm going to do about a funeral later." Dube hung up without saying good-bye.

She called Alexandra with the news, cleaning it up a little. The poor child was getting odder and odder; Catherine's death could just possibly push her over the edge. Alexandra was becoming more uncommunicative. Julia wondered how long she would be able to work, to live alone.

Chapter 7

After Julia hung up, Alexandra thought of nothing else but that she was free to seek her baby daughter. The threat of Catherine killing her no longer existed. She was dead and soon to be buried.

She imagined what her mother's state of mind had been at the end. She was insane, of course. No one can cut their wrists, watch the lifeblood flowing out, coagulating on the floor, and be sane. Alexandra imagined the ebb of life, what were once breathing lungs—taking oxygen out of the atmosphere and utilizing it to feed the cells and then in turn, the organs—slowly diminishing. Blood needed to carry oxygen was wasted as it drained to the floor. Hemoglobin, the matter which transports the oxygen, flowed out of the radial artery; she'd cut both, both hands almost severed from the forearms. Alexandra could imagine her mother, maybe mumbling something unintelligible, or lucid, making the decision to take her own life because of its worthlessness. She wondered if there had been a plan, or if it had been extemporaneous. Was her mother even capable of planning her own death? She thought not. She was probably tired that day, something may have triggered the ideation of cutting, she put her hand to a weapon and did the deed.

The next day, Alexandra was still numb. She felt a small but present tickle at the back of her brain, similar to what she'd felt the day she approached the shack so many years ago, and knew in her heart of hearts that baby Elizabeth would not be there.

She was aware of the effort it would take for those responsible for her to arrange the trip back to New Orleans and coverage for her patients. Left to her own devices, she would have simply run all the way home. She could do it, that was for sure.

She managed to get through the day, focusing on each task as it presented itself. She plodded along, going from exam room to exam room, mumbling facts to sufferers, trying to keep her eyes opened when closing them and feeling her way along the walls of the office was what she wanted to do. She wanted to get out of there so badly. She felt that if she could just find her way back to New Orleans, she would go door to door, street by street, and soon, she'd find her daughter.

She imagined her tiny body, dressed in a small white T-shirt, a cloth diaper, little booties, wrapped tightly in a square of fabric, sucking wildly on her fingers. She sat in her office in a daze, able to smell the flesh of her baby daughter. The repressed memories of the past years came flooding back. Her breasts began to tingle. She remembered holding the tiny, down-covered head up to her chest, the small, rosebud mouth rooting at the young breast, latching on to the nipple, sucking and pulling until liquid began to flow from it.

Alexandra, sitting in the privacy of her office, gripped the arms of her chair. Eyes closed, she saw it all in seconds, lived through those wonderful moments, three months of joy, of ecstasy. And then, nothing. She began to shake. Her entire body, from her feet to the top of her head, tremored. The chair she sat in shook. The rattling alarmed her office staff, who came running, and in shock, thinking she was having a seizure, grasped her and tried to lower her, still in the chair, to the floor. Barely aware of what was happening, but knowing it was no seizure, just an anger remembered, an anger that had multiplied exponentially, she spewed out unintelligible words, but finally, an "I am okay. Please leave me alone."

They ignored her until her savior, May, came to her rescue and shouted, "Stop!" They uprighted her chair, May patting Alexandra's head, the others trying to show compassion and not wanting to leave her. The terrible shaking had stopped. Alexandra was unable to control herself any longer, however.

"Can I leave now? Can I get on the plane?" she asked querulously. "I have to get out of here."

Thinking she was simply despondent about losing her mother, May and Randy gave her permission to leave. May asked her to wait for one moment; she would get her boarding pass for the flight to New Orleans in the early morning. She would be home in plenty of time for the funeral; May thought that was the source of the terrible anguish.

Alexandra allowed herself to be led by May. As May helped her take her lab coat off, Alexandra practiced deep breathing. She closed her eyes. She tried to remember where her running clothes were, how she had gotten to work that morning. May, as if reading her mind, reached behind the door of the doctor's office and grabbed a gym bag.

"James is waiting for you, Doctor. Let him take you the short way home. You can change into your sneakers when you get there and have a nice, long run. Here, I'm going to put these papers into your briefcase. Remember, you need to have your ID when you board." She pushed Alexandra gently toward the elevator, knowing the doctor would rather take the stairs that led to the parking lot. May had a ton of calls to make now; the day wasn't half over. Randy would see the rest of the patients today, but they would have to be rescheduled so they could see an attending surgeon. Whatever else was on the calendar would have to wait. Thank God, it was Friday.

Chapter 8

It took all of Alexandra's self-control not to shake off the clinging hand of May. She was grateful to her for the work it must take to reschedule everything. But it ended there. She didn't care if her outburst was inappropriate, if she looked like a lunatic. She just wanted to be outside, out of the walls closing in on her. Getting onto the elevator was hell. She took shallow, silent breaths between open lips. The urge to scream, to bang on the sides of the box, almost overpowered her, but the doors opened just in time. She bolted out of the elevator, her gym bag and briefcase banging on the sides of the doors.

Through the glass doors at the end of the long corridor she could see the black vehicle with James, waiting. Standing next to him was her main jailer, Peter Van Sant. Informed of her meltdown just minutes ago, he said nothing to her, but stepped aside as James opened the door to the car, taking her bags and throwing them into the front seat. Once she was safely ensconced in the car, though, Peter either couldn't resist or was genuinely concerned.

"Don't worry about a thing, Dr. Donicka. We will take care of everything here; you just take as long as you need, all right?"

She ignored him, as he expected. *Asshole.* He waited for a fraction of a second, and when she didn't respond, tapped the roof of the car. James sped off.

Alexandra sat back against the cool of the vinyl. She kept her eyes closed. She felt the lurch of the car as it made a U-turn to go south on First Avenue. James liked to drive fast. She was glad. She felt the muscles in her neck start to tense up. She knew her mouth would stretch into a grimace if she didn't do some quick quad sets. It was a trick taught to her by a trainer the hospital employed for her. If she was unable to run, she could delay the onset of a facial tic or an all-out spastic attack by contracting muscle groups. The large muscles of her legs and buttocks first; they took the edge off her tension; then her fists and arms, her calves, but not her feet. Once, she did her feet, and the cramping was horrible. When she was done with her muscle groups, she felt the car lurch to the right. They would be on her street. She opened her eyes. She felt the hysteria bubbling up in her throat.

James looked in the rearview mirror, saw her wide, frightened eyes, the expression of terror on her face.

Quickly he said to her, "We're almost there, miss, three seconds." True to his word, he came screeching up to her building, illegally parking in front. He hopped out with her bags and opened her door. She bounded out, grabbing her bags from him. She wanted to thank him for the first time, her lips barely able to open to get the words out. But he knew.

Taking the steps two at a time, she crashed into the door. Struggling with the keys, she managed to get it opened, went through it, slamming it shut behind her. The same scene repeated as she went up to her second-floor apartment and through the door. She threw her bags across the floor. Struggling to get out of her clothes, she tore at the buttons. Her phone rang, and she ignored it.

She set out, fully prepared for a night of running, back up First Avenue past the hospital, the United Nations, under the

Queensboro Bridge, into Harlem, and onto 124th, which she would take across town. She ran through the campus of her old alma mater, down through the Upper West Side, onto Broadway. She would stay on Broadway until she was almost home. Minutes passed, and she felt some life returning to her. Although it was still a long way from what a normal person would feel, she at least was able to take a relaxed breath. She could feel her facial muscles relaxing. No one looked at her a second time; she appeared like any other runner. She came to the bus station and started to slow down. This part of town offered a person the most anonymity. Vagrants and tourists abounded; she melted in, unobserved.

Finally, she could go home. She ran down Twenty-Third to Eighth. The coffee shop was open; she wondered what time it was. She had just completed a marathon. A cup of coffee would be a treat. The owner was there, and he recognized Alexandra, knowing it would be futile to try to engage her. She asked for a double espresso. He wanted to tell her it was eight at night, but she was an adult. If she wanted to stay up all night, that was her business. She pulled some soggy bills out of her waistband pocket. He grimaced, but took them. She didn't notice.

"See you tomorrow," he said sarcastically.

She ignored him or didn't hear it. He never knew with her. She had the reputation of being the neighborhood weirdo; everyone knew she was a brain surgeon, too. But she was a faithful weirdo; every day without fail, she bought something to drink from his store. Sometimes she spoke, but more often, she pointed, not making eye contact or even looking up. He wondered how she managed to take care of patients, hoping he never had to have any brain surgery. She slowly turned to the door, sipping the hot, woodsy liquid. It burned her upper lip, and the little she'd slipped into her mouth, she spit back into the cup through the slit in the lid. She'd let it cool.

She crossed the street, jaywalking to her apartment. She took her time getting up the steps this time, dreamily slipped the key into the lock and turned it, and walked up a flight of stairs to her door. She opened the door easily. Loren had been there and picked up the clothes she'd thrown, but she didn't notice. She didn't remember the haste of her entry and exit. How many hours had it been? On the table in the kitchen were the items she needed for her trip: passport, boarding pass and cash. A small suitcase, already packed, was on the floor next to the counter. She would take this on the plane with her. The less interaction for her with the airlines, the better it would be. If she needed more clothing, Loren would send it to her or she could shop if need be. Loren left her grapes, a small square of cheese and some crackers for her dinner. She took the plate and her espresso, and went into the bedroom. The light was off. The sun was down, and the lights of the city were coming on slowly, glowing brighter as the sun went deeper in the west.

She placed her cardboard cup of espresso and the plate of food on the sill, pulled up her window stool and sat down to eat every piece of food. The coffee was delicious, rich and acidic; she enjoyed every sip. Wedging her big toe in the heel of her shoe, she tugged it off, repeating it on the other side, then bent over and pulled off her socks. The cool air in the room felt wonderful on her hot, sweaty, bruised feet. A relaxed smile spread across her face, the first one in a long while.

Traffic was steady from rush hour until long after midnight. It was Friday night, and real clubbers didn't go out until late. Groups of young people walked past her building, laughing together. She wondered what would provoke that spontaneity. When she was feeling human again someday, Alexandra might love her neighborhood. There were vestiges of it now—the coffee shop, and her neighbors who continued to acknowledge her in spite of her arrogance.

She allowed forbidden thoughts to creep in as she sat at the window. For more than two decades, she had repressed most of the memory of what it was like to have had a relationship, no matter how perverse, that resulted in a pregnancy. She closed her eyes and thought of having another human being's attention. When she was a medical student, maternal child health was hell. Every pregnant woman she had to interview was an enemy. Their purpose was to rub acid into the memory of that last walk home from school when she would discover her baby had been taken. The rotation through labor and delivery was torture. But she endured it. Her instructors thought she was squeamish. Her fellow students protected her, and she got through it.

Now that her mother was dead, she could allow some feelings to return, if they were still available. Were they in her brain? Like the tumors she could see, almost smell? The death of her mother had more than the obvious ramification. Hopefully, now she would find her baby again. Her fears were rising to the surface so she could deal with them. She was afraid of so much. Her mental illness was based in the concept that her mother would kill her baby if she attempted to find her. She'd told her she would. But would she have carried it out? Now Alexandra thought probably not. She'd wasted so much time as the result of a lie.

She sat in the black window, looking out upon the city for hours. New York had become home to her, a safe place, a prison. The rivers surrounding it acted as barriers to evil, but now she wondered if it wasn't just her own gullibility, that of an eleven-year-old child who then never grew up. Why hadn't she reasoned this all out before? She was an adult woman.

She got up to fill her empty espresso cup with water. Standing in the dark bathroom with her eyes closed, running the water from the hot tap, she hit the light switch with her left elbow. She opened her eyes. The bright glare of the blue-grey fluorescent bulb hit her olive skin. Her wild, curly orange hair, untouched since the morning, still slightly damp around her face from the long run, stood out from her face like a basket of leaves. Her eyes were glazed over, huge and brown, with dark smudges underneath. Her skeletal cheekbones, the hollows under them more sunken from dehydration than usual, parched lips, thin long neck—she felt she looked hideous. She quickly flicked the light off. The rest of the night was spent the same way on the stool, looking out over the city. At six, she heard the lock in the door. Loren came in, knocking on the bedroom door, but peeking in.

"Oh, for God's sake, you haven't been up all night, have you?" she asked incredulously. It was obvious she had. "Okay, you better get ready." Loren stalked off, turning the shower on. She would have to deal with the problem directly today. "Hop in the shower, okay? I'll get you some good coffee."

Alexandra slid off the stool and returned to the robot, forgetting her earlier revelation that she was an adult, and walked stiffly to the bathroom. Loren was banging around the kitchen. She was talking loudly into the phone in Spanish, probably complaining. Alexandra went through the motions of bathing, brushing her teeth, her hair, pulling on the clothes Loren had laid out for her. She wasn't even aware of what she had chosen. It didn't matter.

Loren poured out coffee for her employer. She made her a substantial breakfast. May made sure to order a meal for her in flight.

She called Alexandra in to eat. "Did you run this morning?" she asked.

Alexandra stopped eating with her fork poised in the air. She'd forgotten to go out that morning.

"No, I didn't," she said, frowning. "I forgot."

"I'm not surprised, with everything you have going on. Maybe you just needed a break."

Alexandra didn't tell her about the marathon plus run she did after work. But it had never prevented a morning run in the past. While she ate, Loren gave her more instructions about the trip, what to do when she got to security, who to look for if she was having trouble finding her gate. If the words penetrated, Alexandra gave no indication. The buzzer rang. James would be downstairs, waiting to take her to the airport.

It was during the ride to the airport that Alexandra came to her senses. She was on her own now and needed to pull it together, to stop acting like a fool. She had never called Julia, either. For a moment, she wondered how she would get to the museum once she landed. She didn't know if she remembered the address. She could feel the tension growing in her body, her face getting tighter and tighter. This was no time for a grimace. She wanted to be independent. If she blew this trip, it would be the last time she would travel alone, if she was ever allowed on a plane again. So much rested on this one day.

ॐॶ

Usually the view out the car window was lost on Alexandra. She would be deep in empty thought, her mind a blank. She began to think about her old hometown. New Orleans was a big city, in some ways very much like New York. When she ran, the smells of the streets filled her head. She didn't mind smells. Urine, unwashed body, rotting food, flowers, or fish, she recognized them but didn't differentiate. New Orleans had the same smells. Running through the French Quarter was hazardous because odors would linger under the slate of the sidewalks. If a loose slate was harboring water from an early morning washing, a misstep on the edge of the wobbly piece brought hidden foul liquid splashing on her legs. She didn't care, but if it was urine laden, she would hear about it from her teachers, who complained all day that she stunk.

The car came to a stop in the darkness of the Holland Tunnel. Traffic. The exhaust smell was choking. She leaned back against the seat and closed her eyes. She felt the scratchy sensation of lack of sleep behind her eyes. Her body, exhausted from hours of abuse on the road, relaxed in the comfort of the car.

She woke up when the door opened. James reached in with a smile, helping hand stretched out. She rarely took his hand, but today, vulnerable and tired, she grabbed it to make the exit from the low car easier. She stood in the confusion of the airport entrance, the skycap coming toward them with a smile. James told him there were no bags to check, but a ride to the gate would be appreciated, slipping the man a twenty. He sprang into action, leading Alexandra to a waiting area where the cart would pick her up. James stayed with her until a policeman with a fierce look and a ticket book came into the area and he had to move the car.

She sat for ten minutes until the skycap came back to tell her the cart was waiting for her. The driver took her boarding pass and ID, looked it over, and invited her to hop in. She climbed onto the seat. The gate was at the far end of the airport. The cart went fast, swerving around corners, beeping its horn to warn the walking traffic to step aside. Alexandra didn't react, but felt anxious. The people who were walking were so vulnerable. She closed her eyes, willing the walkers to move out of the way.

She boarded the plane without incident. The flight was only troublesome in that the closer she got to New Orleans, the more anxious she became. Julia was the only other human being who knew her motive for returning. Dube, if he thought of her, probably thought she was coming home for the funeral. Nothing was further from the truth. She couldn't care less about the death of her mother, had ceased to even think of her except in terms of the information she carried regarding the whereabouts of Elizabeth.

Hours passed, and the pilot announced they were approaching the runway…

Chapter 9

The Birth

Catherine was mentally ill, but she wasn't stupid. At four o'clock in the morning, she sat bolt up right on the sofa bed with the knowledge that *something was wrong* echoing in her head. Still confused from sleep, she could smell something hot and coppery. Blood! It was coming from somewhere within the shack. Without waiting, she jumped from her bed to the ladder in three moves. Up the ladder, to the room above her bed, unmistakably having given birth was ten-year-old Alexandra.

She had hardly given a thought for the past months to her daughter outside of what was in the house to feed her. She was laying on her back, flannel nightgown printed with doggies straining across her frog-legged knees, white knuckled, with a large-headed baby twitching on the floor. There was a lot of blood. Probably not more blood than is normally present at a birth, but when it's your daughter and you didn't even know she had started menstruating, it looks like a lot more blood than should be there. The mother was paralyzed for a few seconds while she was taking all this in. The light from the lamp outside on the street illuminated the surreal scene, and almost afraid to see more, she hesitated to switch on the light in the attic.

Once she found the courage to do so, it became obvious that the thing wasn't over yet. The cord snaked its way up into her daughter. She saw the fine hairs on her daughter's body that she hadn't noticed before. Her gaze went up until she made contact with the child's eyes. That encounter should've changed the woman's life forever, had she been normal. Terror didn't describe it. It was a look of utter astonishment. If the mother had been out working that night, or never came home at all, chances are the child would have stayed like that without moving for the rest of her life. Suddenly, she arched her body into a contortion that could only mean another contraction was on its way. The mother came to life and moved around to her daughter's head so she could help her sit up a little, help her get in a better position to push the placenta out. Without a whimper, and with a big grunt, she pushed, and the thing slithered out.

Catherine knew she'd better attend to the baby, but for a beat hesitated, until Alexandra spoke. "Is it alive?"

She looked down between her daughter's legs for the second time that night to see it; it not really breathing on its own yet, but alive. She got up from crouching on the attic floor and slowly walked back to the foot of the scene. She grabbed a shirt out of the box next to Alexandra's bed and, with it in hand, knelt down and touched the baby slowly, afraid of it, and rolled it in the cloth. She wiped off what she could of the gunk on the face, remembering reading that you put your finger in the mouth and sweep whatever is there out. Somehow, she found the strength to pick it up and pat its back, and it sputtered, coughed, gurgled, and started to yell. She slowly looked back up at her own child and, again, that face. The look of pure astonishment.

"You've got to cut the cord. In the movies they take shoe laces and tie them around the cord and cut the cord with a knife," Alexandra said, her voice calm and steady.

The mother put the baby back down on the bloody floor, backed down the ladder, went to the cupboard in the kitchen and got a clean knife, found string from some long-forgotten package, and went back up to Alexandra. She performed the task at her daughter's direction. She went back down the ladder for a second and third time to get towels and a bowl of warm water. She washed off the legs and perineum of her daughter. She helped her stand so she could get the horrible flannel gown off, soaked with blood and feces that had gone up her back and neck and into her hairline. Alexandra was silent and let her mother attend to her, having no memory of such tender care from her before.

Once Catherine got her cleaned up, she told Alexandra to sit on the bed. She went back down the ladder for a bag to throw all the stuff away. In the back of her mind, the thought kept popping up like a ghost, *Maybe the thing will die. Die on its own.* But she didn't really think so.

ॐ

The sun was up. Alexandra had had little sleep, but she was wide-awake, every nerve in her body taut, tingling, alive. She was sitting on her bed, next to a little doll. She knew what was going on. She was still a little confused because the whole process of conception and pregnancy and birth just became a reality to her. She was a quick learner. It wasn't when her membranes ruptured, or when the contractions started at lunch time, torturous pain that lasted for hours, not even during the birth, although she was beginning to get the idea. Somehow, because she had embraced the man, the pregnancy resulted. She was both horrified and enraptured by the idea. The details were still mixed up. When she had looked down at the baby between her legs, and then up to her shocked, horrified mother, she knew she'd been caught. She had had a baby. Her own baby. A little child. At that moment, she looked at the little body, and bonded.

The last time she saw her mother, she'd brought her a large white pad for Alexandra to place in her underwear, bigger than the ones her abuser had provided. That was well over an hour ago. Alexandra reached for the baby, who was awake with both fists up to its mouth, eyes wide open. The baby smelled bad, covered in vernix, still wrapped in the bloody T-shirt. Alexandra went to the ladder and softly called down for her mother, but there was no answer. She carefully backed down the ladder and could see her mother was gone. She found the bowl used for the postpartum bath outside on the brick, brought it back in and filled it. She gathered up what towels she could find in the bathroom, a pair of scissors and a pillowcase. She went back up the ladder.

She organized her articles and sat at the baby's foot. She carefully unwrapped the bloody shirt from the baby's body. It was a girl. Some inherent process began, and almost as though she were programmed all her life to care for a baby, she washed and dried the little body, cut a square from the pillowcase and tied it around the baby's bottom, and wrapped her in a clean towel. Suddenly, she felt a tingling feeling at her nipples, and when she looked down, she saw fluid dripping through her nightgown. She looked over at the newborn baby, pulled her gown up over her head, and picked up the infant, who immediately began rooting around. Alexandra held her up to her breast, guiltily looking at the ladder in case her mother should catch her. Nursing didn't take any effort at all. The baby sucked away, tugging at her mother's breast. Eventually, she fell asleep. Alexandra put her gently down and went into her cubbyhole, and found a box suitable for a baby's bed. She placed the sleeping infant in the box and covered her with more towels.

She cut five more diapers out of the pillowcase, but knew that that would not be enough for long. She went back down the ladder, glanced at the clock, and was shocked to see that it was noon. Her mother would have left for work by now. She had walked out of a house where her ten-year-old daughter had just given birth. Even at age ten, Alexandra knew that was negligent. She had always been so self-sufficient the thought of her mother's neglect had never entered her mind until now. She loved her mother. Something just didn't seem right about being left alone. For the first time in her life, she felt critical of Catherine.

It was lunch time, and she was getting hungry. There was a lone can of soup in the cupboard, which she got open, heating up the soup right in the can. That was the easiest way to do it, and for years, she thought that was why it came in a can. Instinctively she knew she better eat and drink if she was going to feed the baby from her body, so she drank a big glass of water and ate all the soup. Pouring another glass of water, she went back up the ladder. Checking on the baby, who was curled into a little ball, she lay down herself and slept.

Sometime after five, she woke up, startled at the sound of a cat crying. She sat up in bed and remembered. She got up to see the baby and realized she better attend to herself first. She went back down the ladder to the bathroom and found the box of pads her mother had, and cleaned herself up. She was first scared when she saw the blood clots, but figured that it must be normal. Washing her hands and face, she longed for a bath.

The baby was sucking on her fists, so she lifted her out of the box, and repeated the nursing routine. She had lots of clearish fluid coming from her breast, soaking everything, including the baby. The baby was greedy, so she switched breasts, and the baby continued to suck. When she fell asleep again, Alexandra untied the soaking rag from the baby and replaced it with a fresh one. She hoped her mother would come home after work tonight and not stay out. She needed to run to the five and dime in the morning. She had been there enough to know that was where she would find the items she needed to take care of her baby.

Throughout the night, the little girl slept and awoke with the baby. She remembered to drink water and to change the infant's diaper. At four in the morning, her mother returned. She came up the ladder and saw in a glance that her self-sufficient daughter had thought of everything, cleaning up, caring for herself and her new baby. She had brought her things from the restaurant: two dozen linen napkins, a huge bottle of apple juice, and a big doggie bag of leftovers. She peeked down at the baby. She put the items in reach of her daughter, patted her on the head, tucked the blanket around her shoulders and, exhausted, went back down the ladder.

She, too, had thought of little else that night besides what they were going to do. It was obvious that they couldn't keep the baby. Thank God, it was June, and the child had the summer off to recover. How unbelievable that she had never noticed, nor had anyone else, that Alexandra was pregnant! She hadn't allowed herself to think about how it had happened, who the father was. She would confront the child later. She suddenly remembered she had never noticed what the baby's sex was. She was so tired. The restaurant had been busier today than usual, Memorial weekend and all. Dube had been after her all night, but his wife was there. She wanted to get him alone to tell him what happened, but Emma never gave her a chance. She had to come back to the shack, after all. She wasn't happy about her predicament, having a child to care for and now a bastard, too.

Shortly after nine that morning, Alexandra bathed and nursed the baby. She'd found the items her mother brought her, and put the linen napkin diaper over the baby's bottom, some expensive diaper it was, and placed her back into her box to sleep. Alexandra dressed in pants and shirt, surprised at how loose her clothes felt, and quietly crept down the ladder with squirreled-away stable money in her fist. Still too early for tourists, she was alone on the streets until she got to Canal. She was surprised how sore she felt, and didn't want to run to the store after all, walking at a normal pace.

At the five and dime, she went to the baby department, got zinc oxide cream for the little red bottom, one dozen cloth diapers because the linen was too harsh, a small bottle with a nipple, just in case, and a flannel baby blanket. After she made her purchases, she went into the grocery store and got a little can of condensed milk, just in case.

She got home thirty minutes later. The baby was still sleeping. She went back down to the kitchen. Craving fresh fruit, milk and cheese, she found brie and French bread in the doggie bag and ate them with apples, then fell sound asleep. The little baby woke her at eleven. She was startled to see her mother standing there, grateful for her silence. Somehow, even though she was a child who had never needed much correction, she knew she would not escape the wrath of her mother.

Her mother said, "You did a nice job fixing things up here, Alexandra." She was still looking at the baby. "What is it?"

Alexandra, confused for a second, realized her mother didn't know what kind of baby it was.

"A girl." Fear like ice ripped through the pit of the child's stomach. She suddenly knew that there might be a problem here. Fortunately, Catherine decided not to pursue any further questioning because when she looked over at her daughter, she could see exhaustion and fear and panic, a mirror of herself.

Chapter 10

So, Alexandra's life took on the routine comfortably and happily. Julia seemed shocked, but always the lady, didn't say anything that could remotely sound critical. Alexandra wasn't allowed to tell anyone else about the baby. Her world became the baby, the shack, and the little brick courtyard out in back. She spent the summer cooing to her baby, nursing her, caring for her, planning how she would get the things she needed for her.

Julia was generous with her; maybe because of the guilt she felt at not noticing the child was in trouble, she became very attentive, never criticizing the child's mother, but there in her absence. She went out of her way to daily inquire after Alexandra's well-being. She brought fresh fruit and other food gifts so that Alexandra was well fed for the first time since they'd moved. Alexandra was careful to hide the gifts from her mother, who was once again silent around her, able to go to work and little else. Thankfully, she had forgotten to question Alexandra regarding the baby's paternity, but the girl knew it was just a matter of time before something would wake her mother up and she would have to face her.

But for now, days would pass where her mother would not even come home from work. Life was back to normal. Julia had arranged for a layette from a charity group at her church to be made available for the baby. It included little gowns made of pastel-colored flannel that tied in the front with thin satin ribbon ties, patchwork flannel blankets and rubberized flannel pads to place the baby on so she wouldn't wet everything around her. Alexandra didn't like rubber pants. She didn't like anything harsh touching her baby.

On one of her trips to the store, she'd found a discarded chest of drawers and dragged it home. She scrubbed it down and used it to store her baby's things. Its drawers were in graduated sizes, and she first used the shallowest one in place of the little crib she would never have. She lined it with the blanket from her cot, and the baby was just fine in it. One of her most challenging moments came the first time she ventured down the ladder with the baby. Her mother wanted her to keep the infant up in the attic, but after a week of confinement, the heat really getting unbearable, Alexandra climbed down. She became very adept at carrying the baby, dressing her and nursing her.

Julia continued her supportive inquiries, asking Alexandra if she needed anything instead of second-guessing. When the baby was a month old, Alexandra confessed she'd like to have a baby carriage. At first, she assumed it would be something she'd look for at the flea market or even on the street. She didn't think of the actual possibility of purchasing it new. Julia said it was a good idea, both of them silently thinking it would have to be something hidden from Catherine or anyone who knew her. That afternoon, she reappeared in the courtyard with a large cardboard box that had a picture of a baby carriage printed on the side. Alexandra was ecstatic. They laughed together as they tore open the box and struggled to get the carriage out. It was a beautiful, expensive thing.

Alexandra ran into the cottage to get the baby and take her for her first outing. She knew it was unlikely that she would run into anyone her mother knew if she confined her walks to St. Charles Ave. on the other side of Canal. The frail red-headed girl pushing a baby carriage would become a familiar sight in the neighborhood that summer. She went to a park that was empty in the summer evening around dinner time, and she could even nurse her baby privately there. Occasionally, passersby would inquire after the little girl, coo, and fuss over the pretty baby in the carriage. Finally, someone asked her what the infant's name was. You could hear the breath rush from her lungs. A name! As easily as if she had been using the name since the baby's birth, Alexandra's mouth formed the sounds that produced Elizabeth. Just like that. Little Elizabeth.

Chapter 11

When George Dube was twenty-six, he met his future wife, Emma, age thirty, daughter of the wealthy Dumont family. They got married in one of New Orleans' most elaborate weddings. Emma did look the beautiful bride. She was a virgin, too. The wedding night was horrible; Dube going through the motions, the bride too embarrassed and too naïve, needing his encouragement, and him not caring enough to give it. Later on, her mother would tell her that every marriage was like this, she'd be smart not to cry or act repulsed. It was too easy for him to get what he needed outside of the marriage.

The first thing Dube did as Mr. Dumont's son-in-law was to get him to mortgage a giant wedding cake of a house on the corner of Bourbon and Canal. His father-in-law financed the installation of a professional kitchen on the first floor. The huge dining room, parlor, and living room became a series of beautiful public dining rooms. In 1944, The Black Swan Café opened for business.

He had the upper two floors converted into living space, including a private kitchen for his soon-to-be big family. He was kind and respectful to his wife, but indifferent to her needs. She responded by spending lavishly on furnishings, clothing, art, whatever her heart desired. She had no interest in the restaurant business and was embarrassed that Dube insisted on living above it, just like a common shopkeeper. Her father admired him, saying that he should have done the same thing, instead of moving his family out to the boondocks; he would have saved a lot of money by overseeing everything himself. Emma and her mother took extended trips to Europe to buy antiques and art, and eventually, her father gave her a small storefront to sell furniture and paintings that she had imported.

Six years passed, and no children were born. But since the waitresses and their children lived above the restaurant, the big house was filled with people in spite of Emma's barrenness. Dube was in a loveless marriage, but he had a successful restaurant that kept him busy. Something else that attracted his interest was the young daughter of his chef. Catherine was a wild little thing, wiry thin with wild red hair, and smart. She was sly, too. She came to the restaurant every day with her mother, and when school started, she'd stop there afterwards. Her mother died when she was twelve, and Catherine came upstairs to live with the others and started working in the kitchen soon after. But she had an eye for Dube. He'd come into the kitchen and, when no one else was looking, she'd pull her knickers down. The first time it happened, it surprised him, so he ran out of the kitchen before anyone else could see what she had done. The next time, he took a closer look.

By now, Dube had lost the starved look he came to the French Quarter with. Having all he could eat for the first time in his life, he ate heartily, and it showed. He weighed over three hundred pounds. Catherine didn't care what he looked like; it was all sport to her anyway, to see if she could tempt him behind his wife's back. She was showing signs of mental illness in childhood. Catherine was great at deceit, and better at conniving. She was the master manipulator, especially to Dube. She became his confidante, and the only thing she did with the information was use it to manipulate him more. He was taken with her, and lost interest in most everything else. Catherine quit going to school, and every minute they weren't working they spent together.

Then, Catherine got pregnant. Dube was thrilled; it was Emma's fault they didn't have children after all. Dube told Emma that Catherine was pregnant with his child. Emma was furious; Catherine, indifferent. Dube, thrust into the middle of the mess, took on the responsibility of seeing to Catherine's diet and safety. Emma couldn't stand the sight of her, and Catherine delighted in taunting her. When she started to show, she flaunted it, pulling up her blouse and rubbing her belly, or asking Emma if she wanted to feel the baby moving. Dube was protective of Catherine and told Emma to leave her alone.

That's when Emma got wise. She could see the baby meant nothing to Catherine except what harm it could do to Dube's marriage. She decided that keeping her husband was more important than her pride. She began by buying the entire layette needed for the baby, calling in decorators and carpenters to redo a room as a nursery. Dube was mystified; so used to being manipulated by Catherine, he didn't see what his wife was up to. She was being kind to Catherine now, taking her up on her offer to feel the baby move, insisting that she see a physician, even making arrangements for her to deliver in an expensive hospital only the very rich used. Eventually, the whole thing backfired; Emma was sincerely getting excited about her husband's baby. It was her idea that they adopt.

Emma refused to allow Catherine to work anymore, saw to it that her room was comfortable, and that she had the proper clothing and food. Dube was getting annoyed, with Emma so involved and poking her nose into Catherine's affairs, there was no time for him to be alone with her for sex.

"Why not leave her alone?" he complained. "You're treating her like she might break in half if she has to lift a finger."

"Poor George," Emma said. "You won't die if you're deprived for a few more months."

Catherine felt trapped, too. She took to escaping to her room in the middle of the night by climbing down the wrought-iron supports that held up the second-floor balconies, or evading Dube and Emma by hiding in one of the many rooms no longer used up on the third floor.

When no one in the house could take anymore of her shenanigans, she went into labor. Her membranes ruptured in the night. She left a trail of amniotic fluid through the hall, up the back stairs that went to the third floor, and through a maze of rooms. Dube went into her room the following morning and didn't find her. Emma discovered the soaked carpet, following it to a small attic room under the eaves. Catherine was naked, squatting and pushing with all her might. Her eyes were black, enormous, and petrified. Emma screamed, and Dube came running, picking her up and shuffling down the stairs while she wailed and pushed. They got her back into her bed, calling the doctor, who arrived just as the head emerged. Emma soothed Catherine, wiping her forehead while Dube sweated and paced and got dizzy watching the birth.

It was a girl. A bald, red, screaming baby. Dube was enchanted. Catherine couldn't have cared less. Emma wanted to get her hands on the baby right away, bloody or not. They would call her Tess.

In time, the house got back to normal. Catherine stopped sneaking around, started working again as a waitress, and had no interest in the baby that Emma and her mother loved. Every spare minute was spent playing with her, dressing her up in baby clothes that made other mothers green with envy, taking her for walks in a grand carriage.

And then, Catherine got pregnant again. Emma, livid, told her husband this time he should just handle it. She wanted nothing to do with it. Dube considered taking Catherine to a friend of a friend that specialized in such problems, but he would see Tess cooing and kicking her booteed feet in the air, and he couldn't do it. He told Catherine she would have to keep it herself; it was evidence of their love for each other. She looked at him out of the corner of her eyes and ignored him.

She got no special care for this pregnancy, no tender attention from Emma. She didn't even acknowledge it. When the time came for her to deliver, Anne, another waitress, attended to her. She told Dube he had another girl. He went in to see a very scrawny thing, hardly whimpering. He felt like he was betraying Tess when he showed any concern for this new addition to his household. The other waitresses felt sorry for the tiny baby, who they named Alexandra, and her survival of the first years was credited to them. Catherine did what they told her to do for it, fed it if it cried, changed the diaper when it needed it, but the others met all the baby's needs. Anne became the baby's guardian of sorts, overseeing Catherine's care of her, insisting that Dube give her extra money for clothing and that Tess's cast-offs be given to her sister. She became a happy, chubby, dimpled baby, not shy of strangers, holding out her little hands to anyone willing to show her affection. The waitresses included the child in all their family activities. When she got a little older, she and Tess would play together all day and curl up together at night, in spite of Emma's concern.

When Alexandra had her fourth birthday, Emma found out that she was finally pregnant herself, at the age of forty-four.

Dube was flabbergasted, and Catherine was disgusted. She refused to sleep with him for months afterward, which might have made Emma's demand that Catherine and Alexandra move out easier for him to execute. Once the decision was made, he moved with record speed. He owned a homestead that used to be part of a farm, in the center of the French Quarter. The large, old house was the one he rented out to Julia's museum of French Quarter history. It was at the front of a courtyard that had a chicken coop in the back.

Dube had some workmen fix up the old building with plumbing and electricity and moved some furniture into it for his crazy mistress and their child. He never went into it himself, but Julia was mortified when she learned that human beings would be living in the shack. She did what she could to make it look more comfortable, but it really was hopeless. After living in that comfortable old house, the chicken coop was not very inviting. But Catherine was happy to be out from under the hateful eye of Emma and into her own place, and was going to try to make a success of it. The child loved it from the first day. The small, brick-paved courtyard out the back door was her haven, and she felt like she was having an adventure just living there. Dube forgot she existed.

And now, all these years later, he was burying his mistress. He had been her protector, paying off the cops when she was caught stealing, refusing to have her institutionalized, keeping her as safe as he could. She was finally gone. He didn't have the energy for anything these days, just thinking about the stress of the funeral made him weak. He was old and depressed, feeling useless because no one else needed him. He wished he would just die. Tess was keeping a close eye on him, and someone looked in on him every hour or so.

Alexandra and Julia were coming to the café to see him. He was working himself up into a sweat worrying about that; he wasn't ready to confront the daughter yet. She had every reason to hate him and demand an explanation as to why he turned his back on her. He just lay back in his chair and fretted. Who would have thought someone as dynamic as he would have such regrets in life?

Chapter 12

Summer in New Orleans was coming to an end, and Alexandra and Elizabeth's time together was almost over. It had been a rough summer for Catherine. But as the heat abated and business slowed down, as people were closing their summer homes, leaving the lake and getting their children back to school, Catherine thought about getting her child back to school, too. There had never been any fuss getting Alexandra ready for school in the past. She seemed to have her own clothing and paper and pencils, and Catherine looked forward to having undisturbed privacy while she was in school.

During the months after the baby was born, Alexandra quietly moved around the cottage when Catherine was home, staying out of the way and keeping the baby out of sight. She'd take the baby out in back until it was time for Catherine to get up again. Then they'd go back up the ladder until she left for work. Catherine seemed to forget that the baby existed, but for a few times when she came up the ladder. She never asked if the baby had a name, had no idea how her daughter got what she needed for her, and didn't care. This was just fine with Alexandra, who knew that where her mother was concerned, less was more.

More often than not that summer, Catherine didn't come home from work at night. Alexandra would be lying on her cot, or sitting up nursing Elizabeth at the fatal hour of two, and there would be silence. If she didn't get home by four, they'd be home free. As September approached, she started to worry about what would happen when school started. She assumed her mother would watch the baby, or maybe she'd let her stay home, or one of the many children who lived above the restaurant could be pressed into service as a babysitter. All these fantasies helped the child deal with the uncertainty, and she convinced herself there was a solution.

As her mother woke up out of her summer daze, she herself thought of a solution. The weekend of Labor Day was usually busy for the restaurant, but when there was a lull, as Alexandra slept sitting up with a sleeping baby at her breast, Dube slipped away to see for himself. A creaking ladder, whispering voices and labored breathing woke her up, and there at the entrance to the attic was the gargantuan Dube and her mother. How he had escaped navigating the ladder without breaking it and falling to his death was all she could think of. No words were exchanged in front of Alexandra, but Catherine pointed to the baby, and Dube went over to the cot. He looked at the frail child and her sleeping baby with sadness in his face, and Alexandra saw it and was petrified. It had never occurred to her to run away from home, but she thought of it now. Dube reached out with a gigantic finger and tenderly drew it along her chin and then down and touched Elizabeth. He looked back at Alexandra and smiled. "You a good momma, little girl." Backing away, he motioned to Catherine, pointed to the ladder and they disappeared down it. Nothing but kindness, as far as she knew, had ever come from Dube's hand. Now she wasn't so sure.

❧

Catherine didn't return to the cottage until the following Monday. School was starting on Tuesday, and in anticipation of it, Alexandra had laundered and hung out to dry the few dresses that weren't too short, along with the baby's diapers and little shirts and gowns that Julia had given her. She was apprehensive, but determined to stick to her schedule. Elizabeth took a lot of work. She ate all day long, took a short nap in the morning and a longer one in the afternoon.

If Alexandra had to run out for anything that Julia didn't supply, she did it during the afternoon nap. She'd find a way to tell Julia she was going out, and at least someone would be aware of the sleeping baby left alone. Alexandra had torturous dreams in which fires began at the foot of the ladder while she was out and there would be no way to get to Elizabeth, or monsters would lurk in the round window in the attic, begging to be let in to get the baby. Alexandra took to sleeping sitting up in the cubbyhole with Elizabeth on her lap. She didn't like to go shopping with the baby because it meant leaving the carriage outside, and on more than one occasion, she'd come out and find pigeons sitting on the hood, or teenage boys getting ready to abscond with it.

She was becoming more and more exhausted but still enjoying motherhood, every thought going to Elizabeth's well-being and comfort. So, when Catherine returned two days later with shopping bags in hand, smiling, Alexandra forgot to be frightened and suspicious for one moment and, with a childish glee, ran to see what was in the bags. Catherine handed them over, and just like a child at Christmas, Alexandra tore into them with delight. In the bags, she found new white panties and T-shirts—even though nursing a three-month-old baby, Alexandra's little breasts didn't require a bra—stockings, several cotton dresses, sweaters, shoe boxes, dusting powder, and sanitary napkins. There were also gifts meant to appease guilt, although the child didn't know that yet: baby clothes, blankets, rattles, little booties. What the woman thought the baby was wearing up to this point in time was a mystery; she didn't know about the gifts from Julia.

It looked like her mother was going to stick around for a while, so Alexandra took a bath, washing out her waist-length, red hair and, with her mother's help, combed all the snarls out and braided it. They bathed the baby together in the sink, a first for Elizabeth, who got the bowl bath every day because Alexandra was afraid of hitting the baby's head on the porcelain. Alexandra assumed that her mother would watch the child the next day when she returned to school. She was nervous about what would happen to her breast milk.

She had once mixed sugar and a grain of salt into canned milk, boiled it, and placed it into the one baby bottle at the direction of Julia as a supplemental feeding when the baby was fussy. She self-consciously prepared it while her mother watched so there would be a meal for Elizabeth while school was in session. No advice or criticism was offered, Catherine's eyes following the child as she performed these tasks so efficiently. Alexandra moved to the chest of drawers, the larger bottom drawer now in service as the baby crib, and removed clothes for her baby daughter's first day away from her young mother. Catherine had never noticed the chest before this moment, but took note of it in her mind, thinking logically for the first time in months that this might be hard to dispose of before the end of the next day came.

Tuesday dawned hot and humid like any autumn day in New Orleans. Alexandra was up early nursing Elizabeth, getting ready for their first day apart. She whispered love songs to her and kissed her fingers and toes. She was looking forward to going back to school. Last year was agonizing. She had been pregnant throughout the whole school year, although at the time she didn't know it, never feeling right, horribly sick to her stomach the first months, then uncomfortable during the last, her teacher looking at her curiously but never too closely.

Somehow, she had survived, and the outcome was this marvelous treasure that meant everything to her. Never had she felt so loved or needed by anything. Her eleventh birthday had come and gone without acknowledgement. She had just forgotten it. It wasn't important. But school was. It meant she was continuing to improve herself for her baby daughter.

By eight Catherine was up. It was unusual for her to see this time of the morning unless she had been up all night. She called up to her daughter to come down and please bring the baby down the ladder for her; it was time she ran off to school. Alexandra slowly climbed down with her three-month-old baby in her right arm, happy, but nervous. She handed Elizabeth off without hesitation; she was as excited about the first day of school as any other eleven-year-old girl would be. A quick kiss to her baby's cheek and she skipped out the door, no more instructions for the baby's care offered or thought of.

She ran to school, the old Alexandra back again, braids flapping in the breeze, no thoughts of anything but sudden carefree exuberance. She didn't know the reason for her light and happy heart, just accepted it as part of the excitement of returning to school. The morning brought reunion with the other students, and she forgot about the baby.

After lunch, the sense of well-being would end. Alexandra had worn an extra T-shirt under her cotton dress just in case her breasts started to leak, but that precaution didn't help. She'd brought a sweater with her, in spite of the heat, and had to put that on. For the rest of the afternoon, she thought about the baby. She wondered if Elizabeth was okay or missed her or minded the bottle of boiled milk, while she was miserable with the heat and the damp cotton drying hard and sticky.

As soon as the bell rang at three, she sprinted out of school as fast as she could and ran back to the shack. The very moment she entered the front courtyard, she relaxed at the prospect of seeing Elizabeth again. She found the front door locked, which was not what she expected, but she pulled up the mat in front of the door and got the key out and let herself in. She knew something was wrong as soon as she crossed the threshold. She ran to the back courtyard to see that the carriage was gone, turned back around and saw that the chest of drawers was gone as well. The baby bottle, gone. Up the ladder to the attic, the drawer, gone. Baby powder, lotion, and stacks of neatly folded diapers, all gone. She flew down the ladder, the last five rungs skipped, and jumped to the floor, landing on her knees. She got up, ran out the front door, looked from side to side to see if she missed anything, and began to scream. Her voice rang out over the rooftops, into the museum, and down the street. Julia ran out of the museum to see what the problem was, but knew as soon as she looked at the child. The baby was gone.

Alexandra was crazed. She ran as fast as she ever had, down St. Francis to the street where the restaurant was, not caring that tears were streaming down her face, forgetting that her mother had forbidden her to ever come into the restaurant when customers were there. Catherine had her back to the front door and didn't see her come in. Alexandra waited behind her silently, the patrons one by one turning their heads to look at the sad little girl, until the woman herself felt the presence behind her and turned around to face her child. Quickly she grabbed the girl by her arm and hustled her out of sight of the diners, into a hallway that led to the familiar rooms above.

"You know better than to come here when I'm working, Alexandra." Her quiet madness confused the child for a moment, she almost apologized, but in seconds remembered why she was there.

"Where's Elizabeth, Momma?"

Catherine tightened her grip on her and pushed her up against the wall.

Hissing at her through clenched teeth, she said, "Don't say another word about the baby, Alexandra. Go about your business, don't try to find her, and she will be safe. If you *ever* mention her again to me or anyone else, you'll be sorry. Babies are easy to kill. Did you know that? Now go home, go back to the shack, and I don't want you to ever come into this restaurant again while customers are here. Do you hear me?"

Choking back hiccupping sobs, Alexandra relaxed under her mother's painful grip and let herself be led silently through the kitchen, eyes there averted, and into the alley behind the restaurant. Catherine pushed her out onto the pavement with such force that she landed on her side, her dress flying up. Turning back, she slammed the door after her.

Alexandra got up and slowly walked out into the street again, this time without purpose, mucous and tears streaming down her face, overwhelming sorrow cruising through her body. For the second time in just over a year, she had lost someone who had become her life, with no recourse. She didn't doubt that her mother was capable of killing Elizabeth, and she wasn't about to test her. She supposed Dube had something to do with it, but he would never betray her; Catherine could make his life miserable. She walked down to the river and sat on one of the benches, maybe the same one that she and the stable worker had sat on. The sun went down, and streetlights came on, and finally she roused herself to get up and walk back to Jackson Square.

Julia was waiting for her, nervous, knowing she was treading on dangerous ground by interfering. She had already admonished herself for sitting back while the child was neglected and obviously molested. Alexandra didn't acknowledge her presence. She had left the door wide open when she fled the first time, and it was still open when she returned.

"If I can help you in any way, I will," Julia said. "I'm so sorry not to have helped you before."

The child didn't seem to hear what was being said to her. She moved to close the door, and Julia backed out of the shack. Alexandra could hear her apologizing again as she shut the door. She slowly walked to the ladder and made her way up to the attic. She took off her dress and T-shirts, wet with milk. Her breasts were beginning to leak again. She put a flannel nightgown on, in spite of the heat, and lay down on her cot. Elizabeth would be getting hungry. She felt helpless and hopeless. She was eleven years old, and her mother knew best. She had taken her baby away without giving the child a chance to say goodbye. She would find the strength, although she didn't know that was what she was looking for, to survive until she was old enough to defy her mother. She would find her daughter again someday. She had to believe this, or die.

The following day, Alexandra found her resolve. Her mother hadn't come home that night. She was glad; it meant not having to face her and fake submission. She rose from her cot and washed her body. Her breasts were hard as rocks and sore. She didn't allow herself to dwell on the reason why. She dressed in layers again and went down the ladder to use the toilet. Julia was standing on the other side of the door when Alexandra came out of the closet. She didn't think it would serve any purpose to be rude; she'd been generous when Elizabeth was born, so she opened the door out of gratitude for that alone. Julia had a small vile of pills in her outstretched hand.

"Dear, if you take one of these pills twice a day for five days, your milk will dry up."

Alexandra accepted the pills from Julia and took pity on her. After all, it wasn't her fault Elizabeth was gone, and she couldn't have prevented it anyway.

"Thank you," she said. She'd think of some way Julia could help her. She would make her an ally. There was no one else.

Chapter 13

The previous morning after Alexandra left for school, Catherine got to work. She stuffed all the baby items, clothes, and neatly folded and stacked diapers that were not much more than rags but clean and white into a woven raffia bag the girl had found somewhere. She threw it down into the main room and climbed down, aware that her daughter, only eleven years old, took the trip up and down the ladder with an armload of baby several times a day. The rest of the junk, the makeshift crib and rickety dresser, she'd get rid of as soon as the baby was gone.

The buggy was ready at the front door. She placed all of the belongings into it and then wedged the baby in last. The little face was clearly questioning. Her mother always spoke sweetly to her, and this person hadn't made eye contact or spoken a word.

Catherine looked out of the window facing the courtyard to see if Julia was in sight. That busybody was the last person she needed to deal with. When she was certain the courtyard was clear, she opened the door and pushed the carriage through it while struggling to hold the door open. Going across the cobblestones in almost a sprint, the baby being bounced and jarred, she ran to the restaurant.

Dube was in the alley, speaking to a deliveryman, when he saw Catherine. *Oh, what now*, he thought. She spotted him and pushed the buggy into his body, his belly rolling from side to side at the impact. Her face contorted. Dube said a silent prayer that she wouldn't do anything more to embarrass him. The deliveryman hopped in his truck and drove off after saying a hurried goodbye. Dube's women problems were famous throughout the food distribution community.

"What's this?" he asked stupidly. He had agreed to find a home for the baby, but in his time.

"Alexandra's," she said flatly.

"Alexandra's what?" he said, knowing he was egging her on and that it might not be pretty.

"Her bastard! What!" Catherine spit and shoved the buggy against him again, turned, and ran away from him.

The baby finally started to cry at the last jar. She was spoken to in only the softest of voices, never handled roughly or ignored, and knew her first pain. It took just a few seconds to work up into a frenzy. Dube swiftly picked her up, more agile than his bulk would attest, hoping to sooth her before the kitchen help heard, or worse, his wife. He needed to keep her as far from this as possible. But it was too late. He heard her before he saw her barrel through the door.

"What's this?" she echoed him. He handed Elizabeth over to his wife, who held her out in front, pinkie fingers raised, with a grimace on her face. *Another bastard of his to take care of,* she thought.

He saw the look and quickly shouted, "It's not mine, for Christ sake! It's the little girl's."

"You tell me an eleven-year-old girl gave birth to this baby? Where the hell has her mother been? She is an idiot, I tell you; it's her baby," Emma said and sneaked a look at the baby anyway. *There it was—copper hair, just like her godforsaken mother and grandmother. And a full head of it, too. Shanty Irish, just like all the rest.*

She'd already forgotten Dube, who snuck away. The hatred welled up in her chest. Best be rid of the thing before she had to feed it, too. She went into the kitchen, and no one looked up, a sure sign that the conversation was overheard. No one had time, energy or money to raise another child. Possibly if money was involved… The wife passed the baby over to a porter, Emmanuel, who hesitated, pulling his hands behind his back in a childish gesture.

"Just hold it, will you? I'm not asking you to nurse it." She went into the empty dining room and called out for her husband, knowing he had escaped to his office.

He was just getting comfortable, having lowered his bulk onto a chaise. His feet hurt, and they had a long night ahead of them. A few minutes with his eyes closed would make it easier.

"Give me some money," she said.

"What! What now!" he cried.

"I need money to get rid of that baby," Emma replied.

Dube struggled to sit up, digging into his back pocket for a wad of money secured with a money clip. He peeled bills off the bundle and threw them onto the floor.

"Please, *please* leave me alone," he whined.

The workers who were setting tables for the evening customers had fled. Passionate fights between Dube and his wife were not uncommon, but always frightening. The porter left holding the baby was scared to death. He made a great show of playing with the baby to hide his discomfort. Hopefully, the wife would come back and relieve him soon.

Back in the kitchen, the cooks were scurrying around, preparing for the evening rush. Dread for the wife's return kept all of them from pausing. When she finally walked in the room, she was too distraught to notice the quiet. She grabbed the porter by the collar and dragged him out into the alley. She pressed the money into his hand.

"Take this money. I don't care if you keep the baby yourself or give it away; just get it out of here." She spun around on her heel and walked out, with him speechless looking after her. She was out of earshot before he was able to protest. He carefully opened the door to the kitchen, and the staff was waiting for him. No one said a word at first.

"You better do what she said and find someone to take that baby off your hands," said the head chef.

"You a daddy now!" someone yelled, followed by laughter.

Then, a screaming yodel from the dining room. "Get the hell back to work!"

The laughter stopped. Emanuel hung around the kitchen for another second and then went back out into the alley. The baby was quiet, looking at him. He thought for a brief minute, and the name Jerome came to him. Jerome was his mother's cousin, a New Orleans police officer for fifteen years. He would know what to do, who to take the baby to. He struggled to put Elizabeth back into the buggy, then maneuvered it carefully through the alley, being careful not to jar her or bounce her around too much. She immediately went to sleep.

❧❦

Jerome and Kathy Rodríguez lived in a small cottage in the Ninth Ward, not far from the Mississippi River. Jerome was the first high school graduate in his family. He went to the Police Academy right after and married Kathy, his high school sweetheart, when he graduated from the academy. They bought their house rather than rent as most of their family did.

Kathy worked full time in the local doctor's office, hiring in as an assistant, but working her way up to office manager. She saved every penny she could, planning for that day when she would no longer work, choosing to stay home with her children.

For years, it was the plan. Every month, Kathy prayed that this would be God's timing, as her mother and aunts and sisters and friends kept telling her. God's Perfect Timing. And every month, there it was, blood on the crotch of her underpants. And the result would be the same, heat spreading through her body, shame and regret filling her heart, tears welling up in her eyes.

No one but Jerome knew the truth; when she was sixteen, she'd had an abortion. It was a legal one, done in a doctor's office set up for such things. In spite of this, she'd gotten an infection. For days, she suffered until Jerome took her back to the doctor. He gave her an antibiotic. However, she had a dreaded feeling that she would be punished. Every Sunday, kneeling in church, walking up to the altar for communion, she felt the wrath of God. She couldn't confess the sin to her priest. Too many stories of secrets being shared outside of the confessional separated her from her god. As best she could, she would try to commune with Him in private. *Oh, Lord, please, please forgive me.*

She tried to be a good wife to Jerome, always putting him first, taking care of his needs above all things. She never asked for anything from him, didn't complain when he spent too much time with his friends or forgot her birthday. She cut the grass, took out the trash, picked up his uniforms from the cleaners. She looked the other way when it was clear he was having an affair.

And as often as she could, as often as he would have her, she had sex with him. She threw herself into the act with such fervor that it often confused Jerome. Her passion filled him with guilt. He knew he didn't deserve her adoration. At times, he would try to pick a fight with her to absolve his sins, but it never worked. She refused to be led down that path.

So this life would have continued indefinitely if not for Emmanuel, frustrated beyond words after struggling to get a screaming baby with her buggy and all her tattered belongings onto a trolley. He always looked the other way when young women traveled with their babies and, clearly needing a helping hand, pulled strollers up the trolley steps with a baby under their arm. He sat on the only available seat, no one offering to help him, hindsight telling him he should have abandoned the carriage in the street. Sweat formed on his forehead as he shifted in his seat, the physical effort catching up with him, self-conscious for the baby's screaming.

A woman sitting next to him finally commented, "Sounds like you got a hungry one there."

He proceeded to dig around in the bags in the carriage for a bottle of milk, but could only come up with a pacifier. He stuck it in Elizabeth's mouth. She was so worked up that it took a few moments for her to figure out it was there. He suddenly thought that Kathy may not appreciate the baby if it was making so much noise.

Finally, the trolley came to their stop. Once again, Emmanuel struggled to get the carriage down the steps without tipping it over and spilling the baby and its belongings all over the road. He almost ran down the sidewalk with the carriage, trying to get to Jerome's as quickly as he could. It occurred to him they may not let him leave the baby there or, worse, no one would be home. He'd leave the carriage with its contents on their doorstep, if that was the case.

Gratefully, thankfully, lights were on in the small bungalow. He left the carriage on the walk up to the house and ran up the steps to the porch. Banging on the door nonstop, Emmanuel was in a frenzy to be rid of the baby and go home. He wasn't going back to work tonight. He had forgotten about the money Dube's wife gave him. Was it for him or the baby? Finally, Kathy answered the door.

"Emmanuel! For heaven's sake," she said, amused at whatever was driving him to bang on the door so hard. "Do you have to use the toilet?" She opened the screen door to let him in as he turned around to go back down the steps. At that moment, she saw the carriage, heard the whimpering. She thought, *Oh, God.*

"My boss got this baby and called me to get rid of it, so here it is. You want it?" Emmanuel was walking backward, away from the house; he was so worried she would refuse him.

"Oh, my holy God. Emmanuel, don't leave yet, you've got to tell me what happened, how this happened." She knew that Jerome would absolutely freak out if she didn't have a story to tell him. Emmanuel's words, "You want it?" echoed through her head repeatedly. She slowly walked toward the carriage as Emmanuel walked away from her.

"I mean it, don't you leave me now or I'll call Jerome!" she threatened.

The timid man stopped.

"Help me with this thing." She pointed at the buggy. She uncovered the baby and picked her up. She was such a tiny little thing, couldn't be more than a few months old. She walked toward the house, talking softly to her, looking her over, while Emmanuel struggled with the buggy; for the last time, he hoped.

Once everything was in the house, Kathy looked through the baby's belongings. There was no evidence of what she normally drank, no formula cans. However, at the bottom of a paper bag of folded diapers, she found an unopened can of Pet Evaporated Milk. In another bag empty bottles, nipples and bottle tops. She took the bag in one hand with the baby in the other arm and went into the kitchen. Elizabeth was still pulling on the pacifier for all she was worth, but she was beginning to root around on Kathy's shirt. The sensation was amazing and was doing amazing things to Kathy's heart. So this was what it was all about. This was all it took.

She put the bottle parts into an empty saucepan, filled it with water, and put it on the stove to heat up. She filled up the teakettle with water. She'd call her mother to ask the proportions of canned milk to water after she dealt with Emmanuel. He was fidgeting in the living room, walking in circles, picking up and then putting down things on the table in front of the couch.

"Okay, tell me what happened," Kathy said.

He repeated as best as he could the events of the day. In retrospect, he found it hard to believe Dube was such a weasel, to allow that woman to literally throw a baby his way to dispose of. Although he was ignorant of the ways of women, he was pretty sure that he had made Kathy very, very happy. She could barely take her eyes off of the baby.

"You realize we will probably have to confront your boss's wife," Kathy said.

Emmanuel didn't know what to say to that, but was certain it would mean him losing his job. Right now, he didn't care and just wanted to get out of the house before she gave the baby back to him and he had to start all over again. He definitely knew he wanted to get out before his cousin came in.

"When's Jerome coming home?" he asked.

"Not until eleven. You're safe…for now." Kathy was onto him. "You better get home. Grandma's making tamales." She walked him to the door. "Keep this a secret, okay?" She might need time to convince Jerry and didn't want the family to know her business until she had something positive to tell them.

"Thank you, Emmanuel, thank you very much." She stood on tiptoe and kissed his cheek. He tried not to run out of the house.

The bottles were bubbling away in the saucepan. She put the baby into the carriage, which precipitated another hysterical crying jig, found pasta tongs in the silverware drawer, and fished a bottle and nipple out of the boiling water. She uprighted it, filled it three-quarters of the way with the boiled water from the teakettle and, opening the canned milk, poured the rest of the way with milk. She'd start out with a weak solution and call her mother when the baby calmed down. She was afraid the baby might have been breast fed, the way she was rooting around.

She ran the bottle under cold water until it was cool enough to drink. The baby latched on to the nipple and started to gulp, it must have been a long while since the last bottle. If she had been breast fed, it didn't seem to affect her now. Calling it a "her," she still wasn't sure what the sex was. While the baby was feeding, she undid her sleeper and peeked into the diaper, which was cloth and soaked through. It was a girl. Kathy sat back into the couch and continued to look over the baby. Suddenly, she began to softly weep. The tears ran down her cheeks, her nose began to run, and she looked down at the little baby girl, finally quiet, calmly sucking on the bottle. It was upon this scene that Jerome would unexpectedly come home during his dinner break.

He'd run into Emmanuel at the local corner party store. His cousin was buying a six-pack and a fifth of rum with a wad of cash in his pocket. Emmanuel had a sheepish look on his face. He considered playing dumb about the baby, but being afraid of his cousin, he opted for honesty right off the bat. After paying for his beer and rum, he walked outside with Jerome and told him the whole baby story. Jerome didn't reply or comment, walked to his car, got in, and drove toward his house.

He took his hat off as he came into the house. Kathy was sitting on the couch, in the dark. Just the light from the kitchen shined in on his wife and the bundle she was holding. There was a faint sucking sound coming from the bundle. He walked over to Kathy and bent over her to see what the bundle contained. She didn't stop gazing at the baby. There were wet streaks down her face, but she was smiling. Finally, she looked up at him.

"I don't know where to begin," she said.

"You don't have to say anything. I saw Emmanuel. I'm not sure we can keep her, though, Kathy. We have to call Child Welfare in the morning." He tried to keep his voice soft and tender.

"I already love her, Jerry," she said. "The second I picked her up, I wasn't in the house yet, I knew she was ours. She needs her diaper changed." She started to scoot toward the edge of the couch to stand up. It was awkward trying to do it with the baby and holding the bottle. Jerome didn't try to take the baby from her. He took her elbow instead and gave her a little boost. They walked over to the carriage.

"Here, take her for a minute so I can look for a diaper."

Jerome didn't hesitate and took the bundle from Kathy. She positioned the bottle for him. She reached over and turned on the table lamp closest to the buggy. Pulling out the last paper sack, they went into the bright kitchen together to look through its contents. Although it looked like everything had been hastily shoved into the bag, what was there was clean and had been folded neatly at one time. The creases were there for her to see. It said to her, "This is my baby. I love her. I can't give her much, but what she has I will take care of." Kathy wondered what would prompt a mother to so rashly give up her baby, almost throw her away. It must have been awful, heartbreaking.

❧

Earlier that day, across town, in a formal courtyard in the French Quarter, a small child standing outside of the shack she lived in, with schoolbooks scattered around her feet where she had dropped them, screamed. She screamed and didn't stop. It was a horrifying sound, so nerve-racking, so earsplitting, that everyone who heard it stopped what they were doing at that minute and looked for the source.

It would be a scream that would not be forgotten.

❧

The next morning, after a sleepless night, Jerome got up and made his wife a cup of coffee. The baby woke up at three for a bottle, half milk, half water per Kathy's mother. But it wasn't the baby that kept Jerome up. It was the worry that they would find out today that the baby had been misplaced or, worse, kidnapped. They would have to give the baby up to the authorities, and Kathy's heart would be broken.

He didn't feel like he had it in him to support her through anymore heartache. He wasn't interested in formally adopting a baby, or having Kathy go through infertility treatments. He was sure he knew what the problem was. She probably had scars from her abortion infection. Investigating infertility would mean dealing with the emotional scars of the abortion. It was just too much.

Worse, he had fathered a baby last year with his current mistress. If Kathy ever found out, he couldn't imagine what would happen. This baby may be just the gift they needed. It would keep her occupied. It would take the pressure off him to fill her life with meaning. It might even open the door for him to leave her. Might.

As it turned out, the woman who gave the baby to Emmanuel to give away was the daughter of one of the biggest political bosses in New Orleans history. The authorities gave their best wishes to Jerome and Kathy Rodríguez, new parents of a healthy, white baby girl.

Chapter 14

Alexandra returned to school that day and every day afterward, and did as well in her classes as she did before. She no longer wandered around the Quarter; the excitement of living there had lost its allure. She didn't care that she was left alone most of the time. She never mentioned Elizabeth again to her mother or Julia and seemed to forget about her altogether. But, that was far from the truth. Each minute of each day, the child longed for her baby. She was determined that she would do well in school, and she did. That was the way she would gain her freedom and find a way to her daughter again.

But Alexandra was changing, the metamorphosis so rapid that Julia was afraid she might have a brain tumor or some other horrible illness. Suddenly, she seemed unable to hold eye contact. She rarely spoke out loud. If you demanded her attention, she would look into your eyes, but her mouth would go through the most disturbing mimicking antics, exaggerating the movements of your own mouth as you tried to speak to her. She would stretch her lips as wide as they would go, slowly opening and closing her mouth as if to speak in slow motion with no sound. It was awful. The first time she did it in school, the teacher asked her to stop, but she was unable to control herself. She was sent to the school nurse, a new woman who didn't know the family history, and a call was put in to her mother.

The next day, with a face swollen and a split lip with dried blood surrounding her mouth, the child walked to school, eyes down. The horrified teacher took her right back to the school nurse, who, guilt filled and anguished, called the police. Alexandra seemed in a daze, yet no one thought to take her to the hospital for an X-ray of her head. They never contacted nor questioned Catherine in the beating of Alexandra, whose downward spiral accelerated after that.

Catherine stopped coming back to the cottage after work. Repulsed by the changes in her daughter, she would have killed her by beating her to a pulp if the child hadn't gotten out of her grasp and run. Before she let the authorities get involved, Julia took over the role of guardian for Alexandra. She had her attorney send Dube a letter stating that he should begin paying child support for her unless he wanted a paternity suit to take place. A sum far above anything Alexandra would ever have asked for herself was demanded, and received. Alexandra now had proper clothing, a clean, lovely home, enough to eat, and someone who cared for her well-being.

She continued to excel in school, in spite of being barely able to sit still for more than five minutes at a time. She was placed in the back of the classroom so she could twist and turn, swirling her body around in spastic movements. She lost so much weight, they were afraid she was anorexic. Although she still had an appetite, no amount of food seemed enough to maintain her weight. Julia was beside herself with worry. A battery of tests given couldn't pinpoint an organic cause for her condition. This was before child study teams and school psychologists were available to help diagnose children with issues. Besides, she didn't have any trouble at all learning. If anything, her IQ seemed to be rising. She was reading every book she could get her hands on. She excelled in the sciences and math. Added to the physical problems, her social behavior was putting her at risk.

It was her English teacher who finally discovered what could be a remedy for her unusual behavior. She noticed on the days Alexandra ran track after lunch, she was able to sit quietly the rest of the afternoon. She still didn't speak or communicate, but she was relaxed and could concentrate. Julia met with her track coach and a nutritionist, and it was determined that she would burn less calories if she ran two hours a day than the fidgeting she was doing. The group invited Alexandra in to discuss what they had planned. She shrugged her shoulders in agreement, but that evening when Julia asked her to take a walk with her on the path they had charted, she tried to control the grimace and sat down to put on her sneakers. Julie turned her back on the child so she couldn't see the tears in her eyes.

They took a circuitous walk around the French Quarter, avoiding The Black Swan. With each step, Alexandra relaxed. She was getting so tall and pretty when she wasn't contorting her face. Her eyes were haunting, large and brown. She didn't seem to mind the pace they were walking, slow enough for Julia, who was wearing flats. Alexandra skipped along, sometimes turning around and skipping backwards so she could look at Julia, all the while Julia kept a stream of slow, comforting conversation going.

She was frightened for Alexandra, frightened that she wouldn't be able to help her anymore and that she would be dependent on someone's care for the rest of her life. It was terrifying to think that her condition could deteriorate to such a level that she would be unable to go off to college or to support herself. It made no difference if she was the smartest woman in the world; if she couldn't communicate or, worse, if she ended up like her mother, her life would be miserable.

As they walked up to the museum, Alexandra stopped. "I want to feel what it's like to run it."

It was getting late, and soon it would be dark. The track coach and the others in the group planned this four-mile run with the understanding that she would run it at fifteen-minute miles and would take an hour. At that rate, she would be out after dark. But Alexandra was no slouch. She was used to navigating the streets and alleys of the French Quarter after dark and had been doing so since she was a small child.

"Okay," Julia said. "Be careful." She leaned forward to kiss Alexandra on the cheek, something she started doing a few months before, but the child was off. Julia went into the house and changed her shoes, put the teakettle on, and was just settling down at the kitchen table with a cup and the mail when Alexandra returned.

"Change your mind?" Julia asked.

"About what?" Alexandra replied.

"Going for a run? Did you forget something?" Julia asked, confused.

"I ran it." She hadn't even broken a sweat. In less than twenty minutes, she ran four miles. Clearly, they had underestimated her speed. She sat down to untie her sneakers.

"Well, what do you think?" Julia said. She decided to try to put it back on Alexandra, get her to talk about it, see what her feelings were.

"It was okay. The pavement is uneven on St. Peter's, so I'll have to watch it there." She sat for a while, twirling the ties on her shorts. "Will I be sleeping here tonight?"

Julia wasn't sure where this was going; she had been there nightly for months now.

"Yes, is that okay with you?" Julia asked.

"It's fine. I want to move my stuff out of the chicken coop," Alexandra replied.

Julia knew there was nothing of value over there; the furniture was stuff Catherine had found on the curb: awful, broken-down crap Dube's wife didn't want anymore. There wasn't a trace of anything Julia knew of that could be salvaged. She wished Dube would tear the damned thing down.

But she decided to take the agreeable route to see where it would lead and just nodded. Maybe moving something out, removing all the familiar articles would finalize the move into the museum. She could then make it her home.

"Would you have a cup of tea with me after we move your things?" Julia didn't want her to go alone. There was something creepy over there still, a lingering spirit and sadness. Alexandra was too vulnerable to suffer that alone. Maybe together they could do something with the place. Nixing that idea, Julia decided that Dube was going to have to get someone to empty it out.

They walked to the shack in silence. It was dark, but there were lights surrounding the courtyard and low lights lighting the path. It felt safe enough. The door was unlocked, and Julia allowed Alexandra to push it open; it had been her house, after all. She flipped on the wall switch, and a bare light bulb in the ceiling glowed yellow and eerie. The place could've been a home if Catherine had cared enough to make it one. Julia stood in the center of the tiny space while Alexandra climbed the ladder. Papers shuffled and footsteps walked above in the attic. Julia felt the burden of one who knew a child had lived there and was alone at night, night after night, and then gave birth and cared for a tiny newborn, up in that stinking, suffocating attic.

Alexandra made the return trip down the ladder and jumped over the last three rungs. She had a journal-type book and a sheaf of papers in her arms, and a paper bag that contained only god knew what. Julia didn't ask what it was.

"Anything else?" Julia was ready to spring out of there, but didn't want to appear impatient.

Alexandra stood in the center of the room and looked around. "I don't ever want to have to come back here again."

Julia put her arm around her shoulders, and they walked out together.

The next morning, after a restless night, an exhausted Alexandra got up at dawn, put her sneakers on, and prepared to go for a run. She tiptoed past Julia's door, but took the time to leave a note. *Be back soon*, it said.

The air was cool and damp, and as soon as she stepped out of the door into the courtyard, her hair lifted up into a halo of frizz. When it frizzed, it lifted out of her eyes, didn't have to be braided, and was light on her head. She didn't bother to warm up or stretch, but did bob her head up and down as she bounced along the sidewalk. Conti's sidewalks were cobbled, but she didn't think to run in the street.

When she reached Bourbon, she decided it was too scary to go past the restaurant, so she'd make her own route. She ran halfway to the zoo and back, about ten miles, and she did it in an hour.

Julia was still sleeping when she got home. She didn't want to go back to bed because it would be too hard to wake up again. Going to the sink to get a glass of water, Alexandra sat at the window overlooking the courtyard, drinking her water. The quiet time would become a routine she'd repeat daily for the rest of her life. Slowly, because of the exertion of the run, her mind cleared of the unspoken terrors that haunted her. The ritual would allow her to live a somewhat normal life.

Julia got up shortly after Alexandra arrived back home. She walked into the kitchen, and when she realized the run had already taken place, saw the note and the wild, damp hair, she felt as though they could handle this now; there was a way for Alexandra to have some control.

What she would come to understand in time was that the years of neglect and abuse, and the final assault of molestation, had taken its toll. The resilience of the child would be tested again and again, but the euphoria she experienced at the birth of Elizabeth, the unfettered love and devotion she had for the baby, and then the utter devastation of the baby being taken from her in the fashion she was taken had consequences that would be lifelong and brutal.

Alexandra relinquished that part of her that lay between her emotions and her thought processing; all the characteristics of her humanity hid below the surface. The sweet personality disappeared, replaced with disinterest and a flat affect. Communication, socialization, and seeking companionship gave way to isolation. Her perception of her physical body disappeared; she lost the concept of her appearance, feelings—which included hunger, fatigue and anxiety—and the social values of appropriateness.

The positive outcome was that her intellectual mind, the part of her brain that processed information, where her ideas and creative thoughts came from, was developing at an astronomical rate. She was becoming more intuitive, but lost her common sense about the most basic functions of living. Julia laid out her clothing and then helped her dress when she seemed to have forgotten how to. The solution to most of the problems was to assist her. Julia found that Alexandra could read a list and follow the directions on it, as long as there weren't too many choices. Uniform dressing became the answer for the clothing issue. Everything went together, and the colors were compatible.

Now that her appearance issues were resolved, the kids in her neighborhood made fun of her because she ran everywhere. Alexandra would be a target for derision. She didn't respond to it. Julia lived in fear that she would sprain an ankle or sustain some injury and the old demons would reappear. But fortunately, nothing like that happened. Except for the reminders to eat and the assistance in personal hygiene and dressing, she was able to function independently.

At her thirteenth birthday, a group of teachers formed a committee whose purpose was to develop programs of study for students who were above average. Specifically, they were planning for Alexandra, but in order to get funds allocated for the program, they spoke in generalities until they were off the record. Her mind was absorbing everything she read at an astonishing rate.

Her joints were taking a beating. The gym coach encouraged her to try swimming, but she said she felt like a drowned rat at the end of the first try. But she took to swimming, too, and when it was so hot Julia wouldn't allow her to run, the local community pool had one side available for her to swim laps for hours on end. She would drag herself out of the shallow end, shaking and weak legged, but relaxed.

The following year, at age fourteen, she became eligible to take a class at a special program at the local university for gifted children. Julia took her for the testing and initial interview, and when it was over, the interviewer took her aside and told her that calling Alexandra gifted was an understatement. She had a genius IQ and remarkable intuitive sense, but off the record, he was afraid for her because he thought there was an underlying, as yet undiagnosed mental illness. He thought she might have Tourette's syndrome. But if the school psychologist hadn't picked it up, he wasn't going to expose his fears. He wanted this prize of a student. She'd join their High Achievers Program and take science, math, and physics classes.

It went wonderfully. Since the university was close by, she began spending more and more time there, volunteering in the research lab, washing beakers and filing papers. When they got their first computer, she did data entry for them. The first summer they hired her to be a research assistant's assistant in the animal lab. She loved working with the animals and didn't have a negative consciousness about the ethical implications of using animals to test lifesaving procedures in humans.

When she was sixteen, Alexandra graduated high school. She'd finished two years of college, tuition free. She was striking to look at. The solution to her unwieldy hair was to cut it as short as a boy's. She was almost six feet tall, lean and strong. She went from one lab project to the next, loving the milieu. It was a place where her most acute intuitive ideas were put to use. The research fellows discovered the brilliant teenager who worked in their lab, and soon, she would be contributing to papers and theses, given named credit.

The following summer, she discovered the neuroscience lab. She learned to assist in the operating room, where the development of the tubes, or shunts, that would drain fluid from the brain to relieve the symptoms of hydrocephalus was taking place. Alexandra contributed to the process with thought-provoking ideas.

Her senior year in college proved to be her most successful year yet. Only nineteen years old, she needed to make a decision about what she would do next. Her advisors didn't feel she was ready to venture out of that protected environment. The graduate school research fellows encouraged her daily to join their program, and since she liked the work, she decided to apply there. Julia was relieved. She was not ready to micromanage another human's life long distance.

Alexandra went through the motions of living, each minute of her life regimented, expectations of her increasing daily at home and at work. *The sensation must be comparable to being born,* she thought. Satisfying everyone around you, the pressure they put on you gets firmer and firmer.

When she was out on the pavement, she could think about whatever she wanted. Once, she remembered the penis of the man who left her pregnant at ten years old. What was he doing now? When she ran in town, she would pass by a saloon with open doors and the smell of the beer would waft out to her, nauseating and sensuous in the same breath, because he smelled of beer and cigarette smoke, body odor, sweat, crotch. She would certainly never allow another intimacy like that again.

She thought of the baby, the little, tiny toes, so sweet and vulnerable. She could think of these things when she ran because the tears would fly from her face, unobstructed. No one would know, and it became a secret delight, torturing herself with memories. She heard those who were most concerned about her talking in voices just loud enough. They must have thought she was untouched by their opinions of her, but she heard them, and it infuriated her. Of course she felt sadness, anger. But what on earth would be the point of expressing those things out loud?

Catherine was no longer a threat, but her scent lingered: the scent of harm, of destruction. What would she do to the baby if Alexandra looked for her? Alexandra didn't want to find out. Julia, who thought she was so in tune with Alexandra, had no idea she thought of the baby at all, let alone day and night. Alexandra's drive was to make everyone happy, to succeed at all costs so that someday she would see her baby again. Success in life equaled success in getting her baby back.

At night, she dreamt of Elizabeth's baby smell. She would take huge, deep breaths of the wonderful smell. It was as real as if she were holding her baby next to her breast. She could imagine the baby rooting at her breasts. Her nipples would erect. She would wake up nauseated, retching, sweating. If she could get out without disturbing Julia, she would go running. Down to the river, climbing up the slippery grass of the levee, once tripping over a drunk who was sleeping at the top. She would run for miles and then turn around and run back, hoping she would make it by daybreak. She hadn't been caught yet, although one time Julia was up fixing her a massive breakfast and thought it had been a regular run, not an all-nighter. She didn't notice the red, swollen eyes.

She was beginning to feel suffocated by everyone watching over her. It was a sign she was growing up. The bad thing about being ahead in school was that you would never have anyone your own age to commiserate with. She wouldn't have confided anyway, but it was healthy to complain. In elementary school, she'd had a little friend named Hannah. She remembered going to Hannah's house as a child and climbing up onto her father's lap. In his astonishment, his arms up in the air, he called for his wife, who ran into the room to see what the commotion was all about. Alexandra was curled up on his lap as if she belonged there, but the wife wasn't having it.

"Alex, get down, for heaven's sake! What are you doing?" She grabbed at Alexandra and pulled her off his lap, as though she might taint him by sitting there.

Hannah, a chubby, whiney little child, started crying. She had compassion for her skinny friend. Alexandra ran home to an empty house. It would be the last time she'd want the attention of a man, until her long-haired molester.

There were research fellows who would try to tease her and engage her, but she played shy, ignoring it. Any other teenage girl would have been thrilled with the attention. She did not examine what she was feeling too closely. If she was a regular girl, not a former mother, she might have entertained their interest. But she had only one goal, and that was to be positioned to get her baby back.

"What're you doin' tonight?" Joe Black asked. He was a go'ole boy from Louisiana.

"I'm going home and studying," she answered.

"Come out with us," Joe replied. "We're going to Freda's Café after work." He was standing so close to Alexandra that she could smell his deodorant, a strong, chemical smell that was close to gagging her.

"Ah, I don't think so," she said. She continued pretending to look at microscope slides, not seeing anything, but able to converse like a normal person as long as she concentrated on something else. His smell was making it really difficult to ignore him. She put the last slide down, knowing she was going to have to go back and re-examine every one. "Could you stand over there?" she asked, pointing a few feet away. Then without meaning to, a little smile worked its way onto her mouth. He saw it and jumped at it.

"Come on, Alex, come out with us," he prompted, getting closer to her. She could smell his breath: coffee and something greasy, rank. "It's fun to see everyone out of this lab."

"I can't drink. I'm only nineteen," she said, looking him in the eye. There was something insincere about him; she couldn't pinpoint what it was exactly, but suddenly she knew she'd never go out with his group. They weren't safe. "Please leave me alone before I report you for harassing me."

Joe Black took a step closer to her. "You're serious, aren't you?" he stated. "I'd heard you were a lunatic, but I didn't want to believe it. What's wrong with you, anyway?"

She turned to him again. Then stretching her mouth open as wide as it would go, she screamed.

"Oh, Jesus Christ!" Joe Black said. "Stop it, I'm sorry, please."

Alexandra shut her mouth while she could still control it; just a few more seconds and they'd have to call an ambulance to haul her away. She felt the stress of the encounter with him affecting her legs and trunk, her arms tensing up in spasms.

"Get away from me, Joe. I mean it. I *am* crazy. I won't be held responsible for what might happen if you don't back off," Alexandra said, lying. She couldn't hurt another human being but threatening to might be helpful in the future, she could see. He gave her the finger and left the lab quickly, before she could scream again. After that day, she continued to perform her tasks in the lab, but she knew her time there might be ending.

She loved the operating room, feeling as though the scalpel was an extension of her fingers. She was able to dissect tissues with precision, never cutting too deeply, avoiding important structures. Being in the brain was her favorite. The first cut, peeling the scalp off of the bone with an elevator, using the drill, and then the saw to cut the bone flap, seeing the covering of the brain. She loved picking up the tissue with forceps and cutting it open, exposing the brain. The feel of bone wax between her latex gloved hands, smashing it up against the cut, oozing bone, then rolling the remains around into a ball and setting it aside for use later, the little balls of wax lined up perfectly. She took the green ties, pieces of suture without a needle, and lined them up under a towel, the heaviest further from her, and the black silk ties next to the green. Every instrument she used, she placed a certain way on her Mayo stand. She set up her own instruments, preferring to work that way for years to come. The training in the animal lab had benefits for the future.

Chapter 15

She finally made the decision that she was going to medical school. Her advisor told her weekly she needed to apply. He helped her sign up to take the MCAT that spring. She was accepted to Columbia University. Julia was a wreck during the process, but Alexandra explained to her that she needed to be off on her own. She knew it was risky to be *out there* alone. She was determined not to allow guilt, or poverty, or nerves keep her from taking this step. No one would prevent a doctor from getting custody of her own baby.

She asked Julia to go with her to speak with Dube about money. Julia called him and told him the plan, that she needed money, and he agreed. Catherine's name wasn't mentioned.

In June, she received her master's degree at twenty years old. She spent the next two weeks following Julia around department stores as they spent Dube's money freely on appropriate clothing for a fall semester in the College of Human Medicine. Julia was in her element dressing her, and Alexandra didn't mind. She could've gone with the clothes on her back. Going away wasn't exciting. She just knew it was the right thing to do at the right time. She would survive it, somehow.

Finally, the day to leave New Orleans for New York arrived. Alexandra had never been out of the city. There hadn't been time to visit the campus, and it seemed ridiculous to waste the time going there. Julia was going along to help her get settled in. She was a Park Avenue brat herself, and although she hadn't been back to visit since taking over the responsibilities of Alexandra, it hadn't changed much; it was possibly cleaner, according to her sister, who still lived there. How she would survive the streets of New York was a worry.

Once they got to the airport and boarded the plane, the reality of what she was doing hit. Alexandra was sitting with her eyes closed, but she was far from relaxed. The thought that she didn't say goodbye to her mother popped into her head. She wondered if Catherine even knew she was leaving for medical school. Dube must have told her; it was his money, after all, that was allowing her to go in style. It turned out that she would receive a large sum of money from the college itself. They had gotten wind that she was considering going to University of Michigan, which was a lie told by her advisor, and would've done anything to keep her there in New York. She was going to be okay as far as money went.

School officials knew Alexandra's history and wanted her anyway. Her advisor at college had called her problem a *tic*. They understood that she needed a lot of support with the basic activities of daily living. Everyone in the program knew that she was going to be a neurosurgeon. During neurology anatomy class, Alexandra acted as the teacher's assistant, lab assistant, study group leader and whatever else was thrown at her. The professor didn't hide the fact that he was certain she knew more about the anatomy of the brain than he did. They could take a slice of brain from an unknown area, give it to her to identify, and she always got it right.

The second sight Alexandra was blessed with was difficult to explain without a demonstration. An MRI or magnetic resonance imaging is a scan of the head that creates a detailed picture of the brain. It uses a magnet, rather than radiation, as X-rays or CT scans do. Alexandra was able to look at the images, called slices, and see subtle nuances of shadow that she was unable to see on other types of studies. When she was showing other physicians what she saw, they were unable to detect the differences. She was tested over again using case studies of patients who had undetected tumor infiltration on MRI that was subsequently discovered during surgery.

During this testing, an additional, more thrilling discovery was made. Alexandra could tell by some slight difference in substance whether a tumor was malignant or benign. Her detractors scoffed at this, saying it was a cheap carnival trick, not real medicine, and that it was dangerous, if not downright negligent, to even entertain the idea that a surgeon would use such buffoonery to diagnose, when the only real and true method was to cut into the head.

The four years of medical school prepared Alexandra for the residency she was offered at NYMC. But the change in the atmosphere would test her ability to function. It had taken from the time she was twelve, when she started to show signs of aberrant behavior, to her twenty-fourth birthday to finally get a diagnosis. The psychologists believed that she had a form of late onset autism. The physical symptoms were psychosomatic. The only treatment was the lifestyle change put into place by Julia years before. Intensive, sustained physical exercise and constant guidance would allow her to use her gifts to their fullest, function in society, and have as normal a life as possible.

Chapter 16

After Catherine's death, Alexandra arrived in New Orleans at eleven Saturday morning. The plane didn't pull up to a gate, staying on the tarmac. A ladder on wheels rolled to the plane door, and they disembarked in the middle of the asphalt. The heat hit her full force; her body immediately remembered that humid, cloying heat. She felt sick to her stomach, her bowels rumbling.

Alexandra went down the ladder and walked into the terminal. No one was waiting for her, but she didn't expect anyone. She would take a cab to Julia's, unload her bag, and then go right to The Black Swan. Her audience with Dube wouldn't take long. She wasn't going to leave until she found out where Elizabeth was. The goal of her journey wasn't Catherine's funeral, but reconciliation.

The plan changed when she got to Julia's. Her good friend had already done the footwork. As soon as Alexandra walked through the door, Julia handed her a piece of paper with a name and address printed on it. They embraced, and Alexandra turned around and went right back out. The cab hadn't pulled away from the curb yet. She tapped on the window so he would know she was getting back in. She gave him the address printed on the piece of paper. Sitting back, she opened her bag, took out a tissue, and wiped her face and hands. The cab was hotter now than it had been on the way from the airport. She felt faintly nauseated. She accepted the feeling, hoping she wouldn't get sick in the cab.

She studied the name on the paper. Jerome and Kathy Rodríguez. Colleen Rodríguez. Elizabeth's name. She was no longer a little baby, as Alexandra had pictured her, had referred to in her dreams. She was a young woman, twenty-eight years old. Alexandra bent over, head in hands. *Of course she wasn't a baby anymore. Oh God. Oh God.*

Maybe she should have called first. Let them know that she was coming and not surprise them. Not let them think she would cause trouble. She started to worry, started to think she was making a mistake, but it was too late. The driver pulled up to the house, in the driveway. Someone peeked out of the closed drapes. A timid, small movement.

Alexandra opened the cab door to get a breath of air. She was dizzy. She knew she was responding to the stress. Her body was failing her. She felt a grumbling in her lower belly. She found bills in her bag and threw them onto the front seat for the driver, got out and shut the door. She wouldn't ask him to wait. If these people wouldn't see her, she would throw off her shoes and run back to Julia's.

She slowly walked up the steps to the porch, aware of being observed. She lightly tapped on the screen door. The wooden door opened a crack. The eyes looked at Alexandra with familiarity.

"Please go away," the woman said. She was middle-aged or slightly older, Hispanic. She was probably beautiful in her youth, but Alexandra saw pain on the face looking back at her. The door began to close.

Alexandra swooned slightly and leaned her head against the door. "Please, please don't send me away. I have wanted to talk to you for a long time. I had a baby when I was eleven years old. She was taken away from me, and I think she came to live here. I won't ask anything of you. I just want to know if she is okay. Please. Please." Her eyes had closed. Her body pressed against the screen. She was little more than a feather dressed in a suit.

Pale and sick looking, speaking in a whisper, Alexandra knew she was approaching a place in her life that could turn either way. She could fall apart, pathetic, and be at the mercy of others, or she could take control. It was out of character. A stranger had seen the total woman as no one had ever seen her. Something in Kathy registered that this was no act. This woman was at the end of her rope and lived for the moment. It gave her great empathy. She remembered when she felt such exhaustion with life and that a little baby brought her new hope. This woman's little baby. She should send her on her way, let the fantasy continue, lie even. But she had a feeling that lying about Colleen now would be crueler than telling the woman the truth.

"Come in," Kathy said, opening the door for Alexandra, who stumbled over the threshold into the clean, cool room. She was so grateful for that. Already she felt better; this woman had been able to give her daughter a clean, comfortable home rather than an awful shack.

Kathy pointed to the couch and told Alexandra to have a seat. She couldn't help the edge to her voice. She wasn't angry with her. Was she jealous of her? She was obviously cultured. Her suit was perfectly tailored and of a light and expensive silk fabric. She was rail thin and muscular. Her hands were shaking, though, and she had sweat on her upper lip.

"Let me get you a glass of water," Kathy said compassionately as she walked into the kitchen.

Alexandra followed her with her eyes. When Kathy returned, she took the water from her and put it to her lips. She was terribly thirsty, suddenly. She took big drinks and let the cool water run down her throat. Immediately she felt better. When the water was gone, Kathy took the glass and refilled it. She also cut up some oranges and pineapple and put them on a plate.

Alexandra ate the fruit with her second glass of water and began to feel refreshed. This woman was kind and thoughtful. The woman looked at her curiously; her guest was an adult, but there was something childlike about her. It was something that rubbed the wrong way.

Kathy decided to ask Alexandra some questions first. She didn't have anything to tell her that would bring her joy, better to delay the information as long as possible.

"So you were only eleven when you had her. That must have been hard," Kathy said. She hoped that was benign enough. Not knowing Alexandra, she thought she might have offended her because her answer was a quiet yes. Kathy decided to come right out and not waste time.

"Do you mind talking about that time?" she asked.

Alexandra shook her head no.

"It's not so much that I mind. It's that I don't remember. I was so young, and the baby meant the world to me. My mother took her away while I was in school, and I never saw her again. I thought I would die." She told Kathy she'd never admitted that to anyone in her life. She told her about the zombie existence she'd had after the baby was kidnapped. And how wonderful she thought it was that her baby came to live in such a nice home with nice people. If only she had known. Life would have been so much easier without the worry.

Kathy didn't want to go on with the conversation. She was losing her nerve. *Just lie and show her to the door.*

"What's Colleen doing now?" Alexandra asked. "Is she finished with school?"

She must mean college, Kathy thought.

"Is she married?"

Kathy stood up and started walking back and forth in the living room. She was wringing her hands, squeezing them and pulling on them. Alexandra was starting to get frightened at the behavior.

"Please tell me. Are you afraid to tell me something?" Alexandra was certain that something was wrong. *Could Elizabeth have died? Was she sick?*

"It's just that I don't know where to begin. She is sick, but not the way you might think. She's a drug addict." Kathy stopped pacing and looked straight at her guest. "She's a methamphetamine addict."

Alexandra bent over, almost folded in half on the couch. Her forehead was pressed against her knees. She had grasped her calves with her hands. She was moaning, "No, I don't believe it, no, please God, no." Over and over. After a few minutes, she sat up. Her voice was harsh, choked up. "What happened? Did it happen in college? Why would she take it in the first place?" All questions any parent would ask.

"I'm not sure if it's the reason she's addicted, but I think she's mentally ill. She was never right. I knew there was something wrong with her when she was here just a few years. Some of it was so perverse; I'm embarrassed to tell you about it." Kathy looked at Alexandra to see if she should go on. "Do you want to hear more?"

The sickened Alexandra nodded her head.

"When she was just two, she went into the kitchen when I was in the bathroom, took a knife off of the counter, and stabbed our cat to death. She was laughing and plunging the knife into the cat over and over. When I screamed for her to stop, it frightened her, and the knife went flying. I was lucky to see it coming at me. We had to buy new carpeting and a sofa; there was so much blood. My husband said it was from watching violent cartoons, but I couldn't be sure.

"By the time she was four, my husband's friends couldn't come over anymore because she would expose herself right in front of them. She'd throw her head back and laugh. We have never watched even an X-rated movie in this house. They called her 'Beaver' in front of my husband at work. 'How's that Beaver?' they'd tease. It was terrible. She started in on my dad and brothers, any man who came in the house. Jerome was afraid to be in the house alone with her. We took her to a child psychologist, an endocrinologist, you name it. They asked if there was a possibility that she had been sexually abused before she came to our house, but I couldn't answer that."

Alexandra knew she was being asked a question. She couldn't be sure it was safe to open her mouth, she was so appalled. She slowly shook her head back and forth. "She was always with me. No one ever took care of her but me. My mother was supposed to watch her one day when I went to school, but took her away. I don't know how long she was some place besides here. Do you remember what day she came?" Alexandra asked softly.

"It was the ninth. We celebrated her birthday on the ninth for years."

"My mother was insane. She had some exhibitionist behavior. I'm not sure it has anything to do with Colleen's problems, but it might make you feel better to know you did the best you could for her."

They sat in silence for a while. Alexandra had heard enough and wanted to call a halt to the interview.

"Do you think I could see her?" She wasn't going to ask, but thought she must be in rehab, or jail. It was a spur-of-the-moment request.

"That's up to you. If you want to see a drug-addicted prostitute. She lives in a pigsty with five kids, all from different fathers. Be my guest. I haven't seen her in years and don't care to. All she wants from me is money to buy drugs." Kathy turned to a desk and got a pen and paper. She wrote down an address and handed it to her.

Alexandra was still reeling from the prostitute comment. *It must be genetic.* .

She picked up her bag and walked to the door. Kathy was still standing on the other side of the room. She had been hurt deeply, disappointed in the way her life had turned out. Here was someone she could blame it on. But she wouldn't say anything more. Alexandra would get what she deserved soon enough.

❧❧

She walked out of the house and down the steps. There were no taxis to catch here, so she'd have to walk. She looked at the scrap of paper Kathy gave her. It was an address, but not of a rehab facility or a jail but of a house not too far away. Alexandra wasn't fearful, but she was no slouch. Perhaps if her daughter was as horrible as her mother had said, she shouldn't go there alone, or without a getaway car. She needed to run. She needed to slip on some sneakers and run like a demon. She didn't care about anything else at that moment. The next street she came to had trolley tracks on it, so she knew if she kept walking, she'd find a trolley and get to Julia's in no time. No sooner did the thought come to her than the trolley came into view.

The trolley rolled to a stop, but Alexandra changed her mind as a rush of prophetic panic came over her. What if Elizabeth overdosed tonight and she would never again have the chance to see her daughter? She had the address; she was just blocks away from her beloved only child. Her life's ambition was about to be realized with a twist; instead of the innocent infant she imagined, she'd found a grown-up drug addict. She turned back from the trolley and walked to the sidewalk toward the street where Elizabeth lived.

She was on the right street. A block of run-down railroad houses, one worse than another, loomed ahead with patchy lawns, straggly trees and broken concrete. Alexandra didn't see the despair, however. She was looking for house numbers. She knew she was at the right house because of the noise: a yelling female voice, crying children and chaos.

She hesitated before walking up to the door. If Elizabeth was really a drug addict, any knock on the door could be a threat: police, drug dealers looking for money, bill collectors. Now that she'd arrived, there was no turning back. She tapped at the door and could see the children in the house looking out the front windows. From behind the closed door, a voice.

"What do you want?" the voice asked.

"Colleen, I am Alexandra Donicka. When I was eleven years old, I had a baby girl. She was taken away from me when I was in school and given to Jerome and Kathy Rodríguez."

The door opened. The form standing in the doorway before her was so physically like her, Alexandra gasped. Tall and slender with copper-colored hair and brown eyes.

But there the similarities ended. Her skin was pockmarked and scabbed, with scratch marks where she had dug at the sores. Her teeth were black with rot. Fetid breath came from her mouth to Alexandra's nose. Her clothes were ragged and filthy. The stench coming from the house was overpowered by the smell of the young woman. She was a walking advertisement for methamphetamine use. Alexandra stood paralyzed. Colleen opened the door wider and stepped aside for Alexandra to pass, looking her up and down, mouth open in astonishment.

"So you finally show up."

Alexandra looked at her, surprised. How had she known she was her mother? Alexandra wondered if Kathy had called to warn her.

"I didn't come from those two Puerto Ricans, now, did I?" The young woman was obviously enjoying Alexandra's discomfort, which was palpable.

She stood in the center of the room, speechless. Alexandra just couldn't believe it. This apparition could not be her daughter. She looked around her. In the tiny room were more than the five children Kathy said she had. Maybe Kathy meant she had five children the last time she saw her, years ago.

The children were all ages; the oldest was a little girl, tall and skinny for her age, with red hair. Alexandra saw more girls, younger than the redhead, and several tiny ones, diapered, dirty, and crying. Could this be a day care? She didn't think so. Her gorge began to rise, and for a second Alexandra was frightened that she might vomit.

She was beyond speech. Someone had to say something eventually, but Alexandra couldn't open her mouth. Suddenly, she stepped forward, propelled by an invisible hand. She reached out for the young woman who was supposed to be her daughter. Her arms encircled the skeletal frame. She embraced her, gently patting her back, and began to weep.

"My little baby, my little baby," she repeated. Oh, how she ached inside for her, for the pain she must have suffered to come to this. Alexandra knew there was a familial thing that could be responsible. So many feelings were swirling, she didn't know what to say. She stepped away from Elizabeth/Colleen. The embrace may not have been appreciated, but she hadn't pulled away first.

They looked at each other. Colleen didn't look embarrassed or sad. She had a smirk frozen on her face. But there was a little confusion in her eyes. She was waiting for recriminations from the stranger, but then none came. The stranger seemed sincerely regretful that her daughter had been taken from her.

Finally, Colleen broke the silence. "Sit down." She pointed toward the sofa.

Alexandra bent down to clear some papers and toys away so she could sit. The children surrounded her, quiet finally, curious. They crept closer and closer to her. Alexandra counted eight children, and two of them were boys.

"Get the hell away from her!" Colleen yelled, scaring Alexandra so she popped up off the couch.

Alexandra wanted to contradict her, but she kept her mouth shut. She could see evidence of her genes in each of the kids. She reached out to the littlest around her.

"Could I pick someone up?" she asked, a forced smile on her face.

They pressed in closer. Alexandra's heart was melting, contradicting the urge to get up and run from the house. She mustn't get attached, but how could she not? The presence of the children was the salve she needed not to fall apart from the shock of what her daughter had become.

She looked up at Colleen for confirmation, and the young woman nodded. A tiny body reached up, starved for attention.

Soon, Alexandra had several dirty babies with smelly wet diapers on the lap of her pale beige, silk suit. She couldn't care less. The little bodies were warm. They hugged her, pulled her buttons, twirling her hair in their fingers. The bigger children squeezed in next to her on the sofa. No one said much, but there was a peaceful presence amidst the squalor as Alexandra was transported back to the attic in the French Quarter, nursing a tiny baby.

Colleen's voice interrupted the journey. "I have to run out for a minute. Can you stay with them?"

"Of course," Alexandra said. She knew the young woman was going for drugs. The next request cinched her suspicion.

"You wouldn't have any cash on hand I could have, would you?" There was the smirk. She was the typical manipulative drug addict. Alexandra was the perfect victim, too. She knew it and didn't care. She would give her anything if asked.

"I do. Hand me my bag, would you? How much do you need?" she asked.

"Fifty should do it," Colleen said, as she brought the purse to Alexandra, hand outstretched.

"Do you want to eat dinner together? You could shop for that while you're out," she said. Alexandra knew she was pressing it, but had nothing to lose. If her daughter was lost to her, these children were not.

"There's nothing to eat here. I'll have to go to the store. I'll need money for that, too," Colleen said.

Alexandra dug through her plane tickets and toiletries and pulled ten $20 bills out of her wallet. "Is that enough, *for now?*" she added, looking right in Colleen's eyes. She wasn't going away.

"Yeah, it's plenty. Thanks." And with that, a smile too. *Manipulator.*

Alexandra, who was unable to pick out her own clothes and dress herself properly, got up off the sofa once her daughter was gone, a baby on each hip, and was ready to change their diapers and clothes.

"Do you have any diapers?" she asked the little red-headed girl. "What's your name, by the way? I'm Alexandra."

"I'm Nina," she said. "There might be some diapers back in here."

Alexandra followed Nina as the rest of the children followed her into a back bedroom, picking her feet up over the junk and clothes that littered the floor. She would never have noticed the mess a day ago. It was like her old need for order as a young child had magically returned.

In the bedroom, Nina led her to a changing table covered with trash. But in the storage area was a box of disposable diapers. She counted three diapered children and pulled three diapers out; it would have to be one size fits all. One by one, she bathed the rumps and changed the diapers of three babies. She carefully asked Nina questions as she puttered, cleaning and washing faces and hands. Muscle memory from doing these acts to her own infant came back. Nina said all of the children were her sisters and brothers except for two of the babies who belonged to a homeless friend of Colleen's.

She heard crying from another bedroom. Finishing the last of the diaper changes, she found the tiniest baby of them all. In a crib at the back of the room, a girl lay in filth, her diaper long overdue for a change. Nina said she was almost three months old, the age Elizabeth/Colleen was when Catherine kidnapped her and ruined her life. Alexandra picked the infant up. As she changed her diaper, she caught herself singing the made-up songs she'd sung to her own infant. She couldn't stop trying to make things right for these children. When they were cleaned up, she began organizing the few useable items in their rooms. It would pay off later.

She picked up the three-month-old and corralled the others into the living room.

She called Julia and briefed her, promising to call later in the evening. She'd clean the kitchen and bathroom at the very least. She couldn't use the bathroom in its current condition. The children were hungry, so she needed to clean the kitchen so she could feed them. Alexandra, who was unable to care for herself properly a day ago, was cleaning a bathroom, dressing children, homemaking.

While she cleaned, she engaged Nina in as much questioning as she dared, hoping not to frighten the child or run her off. What she found out sickened her as much as it angered her. Nina wasn't suspicious of Alexandra's questions, seeming starved for the interaction.

"What grade are you in?" Alexandra asked. Didn't every child like to talk about what they were learning in school? But Nina said she didn't go to school. She stayed home to watch the younger children when her mother went out or was sick. She couldn't read or write.

The worst revelation was that she often had to fight off the unwanted sexual advances of her mother's friends, men she was encouraged to call "uncle." Alexandra almost fell over when Nina told her the story. She used words inappropriate for a seven-year-old. Alexandra deduced Nina was raped as payment for drugs Colleen couldn't afford. The last incident resulted in an infection that required hospitalization. For some unknown reason, the child was returned to her mother. Alexandra intended on finding out why as soon as she was able. Her blood pressure increased with each tale, but she didn't think to call the police until later.

The kitchen, overrun with cockroaches and mouse droppings, was the worst. Alexandra wished she had a pair of gloves to wear while she was cleaning the sink out. Rotted food floated in slimy water. She found a plunger and was able to get the plugged-up drain cleared. Thankfully, there was an ancient box of Spic and Span and a roll of paper towels under the sink. She filled the sink with hot, hot water and the detergent. Every surface was cleared of junk and washed down. Papers were piled neatly, and nothing was thrown away unless it was really trash, like old food wrappers.

For an hour she scoured and organized. She wished Loren and Grace could see her work. She'd found bread that wasn't rock hard or moldy and peanut butter, and made sandwiches, opening a can of soup and cooking that as well. With Nina's help, she spooned soup into the littlest mouths. She fed them a can of fruit cocktail. They looked uncomfortable sitting around the table to eat. Nina said they didn't sit at the table, usually eating on the living room floor in front of the television.

The next room to tackle was the bathroom. She gagged while cleaning, but got it so that she could use it. Each child got a bath. She made a mental list of what her daughter needed and what she would do to help her. She didn't care if she was used. She didn't think twice about the money she would spend; she didn't spend any on herself and made a lot of it, so what better use than for her children and grandchildren? She was feeling alive. It seemed such a contradiction to feel so positive amidst the squalor and despair. For the next few hours she learned the names and ages of her grandchildren and told them stories she made up.

Finally, six hours after she left, Colleen came home. Alexandra could smell the sweet smell of crack cocaine on her. She must have had a field day. She had two bags of groceries.

She kept stretching her upper lip over her teeth and rubbing her forearms over her chest and hips, a nervous tic caused by the drugs.

The babies had fallen asleep. Alexandra placed them on a blanket on the living room floor, out of the way of foot traffic. She was worried about mice, but wasn't in a position to give advice, especially not while her daughter was high. Colleen didn't seem to notice the house's improved condition, and Alexandra was glad. She took the grocery bags from her and asked if it was okay if she started dinner. Colleen shrugged her shoulders.

Alexandra put the groceries away. She made cheese sandwiches with tomato so they'd get some vegetables and poured glasses of milk for each child. Knowing she probably wouldn't eat it, Alexandra put a sandwich on the table next to Colleen, who was sitting upright on the sofa with legs up on the coffee table, eyes closed. There was silence as the children ate again. She prepared bottles with powdered formula and fed the babies. She could leave tonight knowing they'd had some protein, however meager.

As the sun went down, the littlest of the children still awake started to yawn. She asked Nina where everyone slept. With Nina's help, she got everyone tucked in. Three little ones piled onto a twin bed. The older children would sleep in the double bed and on the couch. Two babies slept in one crib, the bigger one alone. She got the babies off the floor and into their cribs. She hated to think of the condition of the sheets. Before she walked back into the living room, Nina threw her arms around Alexandra's legs. She whispered, "Don't leave me here."

Alexandra kneeled down and whispered, "I'm going to come back. We need to get to know each other, your mother and I. Let's take it one day at a time, okay?" She hugged the little girl.

They walked into the living room together. Colleen was out cold. Alexandra went back into the kitchen for her bag and pulled out a small pad of paper. She wrote a short note to Colleen with her cell phone number on it. She took another hundred dollars in twenties, all of her travel money, and wrapped the money in the note. She found a rubber band in a junk drawer and placed the band around the note.

On the second piece of paper, she wrote her full name and cell phone number and gave it to Nina. She instructed the child to place the note, with another twenty-dollar bill, in a safe and secret place. She said she had a place in the back of her closet where she put things she didn't want her mother to try to sell. She was only seven years old and already wise to her mother.

Alexandra hugged the child again. She gathered up her bag and pen and paper, straightened her ruined suit, and walked out of the house, first placing the note and cash on the table next to the sandwich.

"Lock the door behind me," she instructed her granddaughter.

The child nodded. She quietly opened the door. Colleen didn't budge. Alexandra stepped out of the door and closed it behind her. She could hear the click of the door. Then she came to her senses. It was dark out, a bad neighborhood, and Alexandra wasn't sure where she was. She was in such turmoil over what she had experienced that day that she didn't give a second thought to her own safety, and was leaving her grandchildren in a house with an unconscious drug addict. What was worse? Nina revealed that she'd been sexually molested more than once. It needed to be reported to the police. It was the law. Calling the police would alienate Colleen from her. Not only that, but tonight someone could come into the house and repeat the acts against the child. She was in danger as long as she was in the house, as the other children were.

She turned around on the porch and could see that Nina was still there, standing next to the living room window and peeking out at her from behind the curtain. Alexandra motioned for her to come back and unlock the door.

"I decided not to leave you now, after all," Alexandra whispered to the child. "You need to get into bed, okay?"

They tiptoed past Colleen into the back bedroom. She pulled the sheets back, and Nina slipped in.

"Try to shut your eyes and go to sleep, my dear. It's been a long day, hasn't it?" Alexandra patted her cheek. She was afraid if she called the police tonight, the children would be frightened. She didn't know if they'd ask her to take them or if they'd be taken to foster care. She thought of instances where someone should have called the police on her behalf. Going to foster care or staying with an unknown grandparent wasn't as bad as the circumstances they were living in. She'd make the call.

"Good night, Alexandra," Nina said. She closed her eyes, obedient.

Alexandra straightened up. She would go into the kitchen and make the call. She didn't want to wake up Colleen.

She went into the kitchen and turned on a light over the kitchen sink. Alexandra could still see if Colleen stirred. She punched in 9-1-1 and waited for the answer to come.

"State your emergency," a male voice said.

"It's not exactly an emergency. It's a long story, but my daughter is a drug addict, and while she was out this afternoon, her seven-year-old daughter told me a friend of her mother's has been molesting her, that she was raped." She was trying to speak clearly but softly. Her heart was beating wildly.

"Is the perpetrator there now?" the voice asked.

"No. Eight children and my daughter, who's unconscious from her last drug use, are here. I'm afraid to leave them alone. I am a physician and realize the responsibility I have now that I have knowledge of the child abuse." She was hoping that hubris would prevent the voice from blowing her off.

"Are you able to stay there?" the voice asked.

"Yes," Alexandra replied.

"What's the address?" Then, "Stay on the line. I'm going to call this in."

Alexandra looked in on her daughter. She was still in the same position, softly snoring. There was no sound coming from the children's bedroom.

Alexandra was suddenly sickened. She lived such a selfish life. She couldn't have known this was happening, could she? Why did she wait until her mother was dead to find Elizabeth? She should have intervened years ago. So stupid and selfish of her!

The voice came back on the line. "Ma'am, are you there?"

Alexandra said, "Yes."

"A unit is on the way. There are female officers coming, as well. Stay on the line with me until they get there." There was some electrical noise in the background.

"How old are the other children?"

Alexandra didn't feel like making small talk, but maybe she needed to know. "All younger than seven."

"Has your daughter been treated for her drug addiction in the past?"

"I don't know. I'm new to the situation," Alexandra said. "My daughter was raised by another family, and I just found her." She realized how awful the story sounded.

The voice sounded sympathetic. "I'm sorry," it said.

Then Alexandra heard cars pulling up. First one, then a second. She whispered into the phone, "They're here. I better go let them in before they knock and wake up the children." She hung up.

She went to the front door and opened it as the officers were walking up the steps, wanting to explain everything to them before they came in. The fear of waking up her daughter, of making her angry and of a scene, was strong, and she didn't want to upset the children.

The officers were polite and listened to her story as she kept peeking in the door to see if Colleen was awake yet.

"You say she's high now?" one of them asked. They were writing down everything she said.

"I gave her money around noon, and she left for six hours. When she returned, I could smell crack on her. She passed out shortly after she got home and has been sleeping ever since. The children are sleeping. What will you do?" She was nervous, completely out of her element.

One of the female officers stepped forward. "You did the right thing," she said reassuringly. "We will have to remove the children from the home. You can come with us if you like. If your daughter is under the influence now, we may be able to get her into rehab." She looked at the older male officer for confirmation.

He nodded in agreement. "We'll call a transport to take her to the hospital. Is that her?" He was looking through the crack of the door at the sleeping form.

Alexandra nodded.

"Okay, let's get it over with."

They walked in behind Alexandra. She went right to the children's room. She didn't want to see them do whatever it was they would do to Colleen—handcuff her or restrain her.

The female officer walked into the bedroom with Alexandra. She bent over Nina, gently shaking her shoulder. One by one, the children started to wake. The officer found the light switch on the bedroom wall.

"We can gather up clothes for them to put on in the morning," she said.

"They don't have much," Alexandra replied.

The officer efficiently went through the drawers and through the piles of clothes everywhere. The babies started to cry, so Alexandra attended to them next, changing their diapers again. She could hear the officers talking in the living room. There was still no sound from Colleen.

Alexandra wasn't used to dressing children or organizing their belongings, but the officer was doing it like she had done this job many times before. The babies were so innocent. She wondered which one wasn't part of the family. *This would give them a better life.*

Within minutes, an ambulance arrived. The EMT workers brought in a stretcher. They got a report from the officers. "The female patient is unconscious from a possible heroin overdose," they said. They gently put her body on the stretcher and removed her from the house.

Once Colleen was out of the room and on her way to the hospital, Alexandra and the officers brought the children out. They explained that they were going to have an adventure, a ride in the police car. Alexandra went in one car, and the female police officer went in the other.

When they got to the station, Alexandra excused herself for a moment. She called Julia and briefly explained what was happening. Then she went to the bathroom. She looked in the mirror for the first time in hours. She didn't recognize the face staring back at her. Unearthly pale, dirty clothes; she must have made a great impression on the police. Then she thought of her daughter, what had happened to her. Alexandra hadn't cried as a child, learning early that it wouldn't make any difference. Only when Elizabeth was taken from her did she remember crying like her heart was broken. It was the last time. She squeezed her eyes, willing to bring a tear to the surface, but nothing came out.

She went back to the reception desk. They had taken the children to Social Services. One of the officers showed her a seat. Exhausted, she felt old and empty. Someone offered her a cup of coffee. She accepted the coffee gratefully.

The officer came in and sat down across from her. She was suddenly self-conscious. It wasn't only her physical appearance; it was that she'd had a part in the sad affairs of her daughter and grandchildren. The worst was forgetting that her baby was growing up the same way she was, getting older every day. Alexandra suddenly wondered what her elementary days had been like, if she'd dated. Who fathered her children? Was she in a relationship with him, or was it a one-night stand. Alexandra's genes, her foolishness that led to the conception, her ignorance at thinking she couldn't locate Elizabeth until the death of her mother. Her stupidity. The officer cleared his throat.

"Do you mind telling me what happened again?" he asked apologetically. She looked frail and exhausted.

Alexandra said she didn't mind and told the whole story again, including how she arrived in the morning from New

York and had her first meeting with her daughter. She didn't hide anything. The officer didn't bat an eye when she explained that she'd given birth as a child. He asked for her identification. When she handed over her New York State ID card, which she had instead of a driver's license, he noticed the notation Physician printed after her name.

Alexandra looked up at the clock on the wall. It was almost midnight. The past twelve hours had gone by in a blur for her. She sipped the coffee. "This is good," she said.

He looked surprised. "I'm glad you think so," he said. *She must be desperate*, he thought. "Someone from Social Services will be coming out to speak with you. You probably won't be able to take the children tonight. A judge has to determine custody, and he left at midnight."

The Social Services person, a huge black man with beautiful long dreadlocks, came to her just then. He lowered his head.

"Miss Donicka?" No one but Loren called her that. She started to stand, but he put his hand up. He walked around and lowered himself onto the chair next to her. It wasn't easy. He was so soft spoken and had a kind look on his face that she didn't notice his size.

"I'm sorry to keep you waiting. I'm Jeff Gaugain. As soon as we heard you were coming in, we tried to detain the judge, but he left before we could get to him. The children will be held in foster care tonight. You don't have to worry about the family; they are our emergency contact and are loving and reliable. The seven-year-old girl is in the ER at County, having a rape exam." He paused to allow her time to speak.

She was speechless, however, and looked at him with eyes beseeching mercy.

He continued. "Your daughter is going to County for thirty days. I heard she is awake and furious. They said you can come in tonight, but I advise against it. Give her tonight to calm down. The officer said you just met her today. What we are reporting is that you called 9-1-1 because you thought she had overdosed. The police are reporting it was a possible heroin overdose. I know you're a doctor and could have called it. She doesn't know that the little girl told you about the rape. As far as you're concerned, I don't think she'll suspect you turning her in. There will be plenty of time for honesty after she gets clean." He sat next to her, patiently waiting for her to respond.

"If there isn't anything I can do for you now, Detective Ryan will take you home. Here's my card. Call me tomorrow if you need to talk. I'll be here until three, back at three tomorrow afternoon." He stood up to leave.

"There is one thing," she said.

He paused and looked down at her.

"If I take the children, they will have to return to New York with me. I have a neurosurgery practice there. I came to New Orleans for my mother's funeral. I'm not sure how long I can stay away from work." It sounded hollow and selfish. "I'm sorry."

"Miss Donicka, you have enough on your plate right now. We understand you have to make a living. Don't worry about anything. That's what is so great about having your fate placed in the legal system. All the decisions will be made for you." He smiled down at her.

"Okay, if you say so," she said. She stood up, taking his hand to shake. "Thank you, Jeff. You have beautiful hair." Saying the words startled her; stating an observation about a person's appearance was foreign to her.

He turned to walk away, but tossed his dreadlocks for her first.

⟡⟐

Detective Ryan had been waiting for the conversation to end so he could find out if the doctor wanted to go to the hospital to see her daughter or go home. He walked up to her.

"Home or hospital?" he asked.

"Home," she replied.

He motioned for her to follow him. Her bag felt like it held stones. She walked a few steps behind him, unable to connect with another human right then. He allowed her the space. He thought she was serene for having gone through so much in a day, or was doing a fine job covering up.

They left the air-conditioned police department, and the heat hit her in the face. It was hard to believe it was almost Christmas. She thought of Manhattan for the first time that day, wondering what the weather was like back home. It occurred to her that her muscles were limber and she was talking appropriately yet she hadn't run all day.

Tom Ryan was waiting for her. He opened the door of the cruiser for her, and as she climbed in, he could see the beautiful fabric of her ruined suit, the expensive tailoring, and the dirt and stains that covered the front of the skirt and jacket. He'd read the report the officers had written, the house where the children lived was a squalor, and wondered what her visit with them had been like.

He asked for an address, and she gave him Julia's street. She was struggling to keep her body upright. She wanted to lay her head back and close her eyes for just a moment. He saw her out of the corner of his eye.

"You must be tired."

She squirmed a little, shifting her position, and spoke like a normal adult woman. "Exhausted," she said. "But it's nothing that a levee run wouldn't cure." When she was in high school, she'd do levee runs every day. Sidewalks on top of the levees made perfect tracks for runners, with gorgeous scenery. She planned to do a good long one, maybe fifteen miles, as soon as she could.

"Wow, you really are a New Orleans gal," he said. Usually only runners from town knew the term *levee run*. "Better wait until daylight, though." He wished he could ask to tag along, but thought better of it.

"I will; wait, I mean. I'm too tired to do anything tonight."

They pulled up in front of Julia's house. Alexandra could see her looking out the window.

"Thank you for the ride," she said as he opened the door for her. She wasn't used to the chivalry.

He decided to throw caution to the wind. "Can I run with you tomorrow?"

She looked at him, surprised, not knowing what to say.

"Nothing big, just a run." He smiled at her, wishing she would relax.

"Just a run," she repeated. She appeared to think about the ramifications of *just a run* and nodded her head.

"What time do you think I'll be summoned to court?" She wanted to get up at sunrise, and probably he'd still be at work. She could avert a date.

"Someone will call you after the courthouse opens at nine. I'll give you a call when I get off work around eight, okay?" He waited for her answer.

She started to walk to the gate and turned around. "Thank you again," she said, trying not to sprint away. She didn't wait for a reply.

Julia opened the door for her, slowly shaking her head back and forth.

"What a mess," she said. But that's as far as she went. She was proud of Alexandra, who'd taken care of a terrible situation alone.

"Thank you for not asking," Alexandra said. She took off her suit in the hallway. "This thing is going in the trash right now." Julia bent down to pick up the jacket when Alexandra said, "Don't touch it. I'm not kidding when I tell you that it is dangerously contaminated."

Julia stood back up. She wasn't going to ask questions tonight. Alexandra finished stripping, wadded the suit into a ball, and threw it into a trashcan in the boiler room of the museum. She walked back into the kitchen in her slip.

"I'm going to get a shower, so don't hug me," Alexandra said. She walked toward the staircase and turned to Julia. "What a mess I've made of things."

"It's not of your making, Alex. You were born into it. Get your shower, and I'll make you tea," Julia said.

A half hour later, Alexandra came down the stairs in a bathrobe with wet hair and a towel around her shoulders. Julia had the teakettle on. The women sat together, old friends who had no secrets from one another any longer, while Alexandra told her the awful story of what had become of her precious baby Elizabeth. She'd been an icon to Alexandra, a perpetual infant who needed to be rescued. But it was too late for her. Something in her genetic makeup, or her environment that was unaccounted for, led her to her current, dire circumstances.

Chapter 17

At six the next morning, it was pitch black out, but some birds chirped loudly enough to wake Alexandra up. She put on shorts and a T-shirt laid out the night before, stuck her feet into sneakers, brushed her teeth, and quietly let herself out of the museum. It had occurred to her again that just two days before, it was necessary for someone else to do those things for her, to remind her to brush her teeth, to lay out her clothes.

Running to the river, she shook her head in disgust at what she had become: a big helpless adult who depended on others for the most basic needs. She felt the cool, humid air on her skin as she ran, the awareness of her body and the emotions of what she'd experienced the day before serving a dual purpose; she was no longer a numb zombie, a robot. She was going through the stages of grief already. She was a thinking, feeling woman, someone who would soon have to deal with anger that was simmering below the surface, anger for having wasted her life. She realized she could blame her mother, her molester, Dube and everyone else who manipulated her, but the truth was she had only herself to blame. She was to blame for losing her daughter. It was all she could do right then to keep moving, to not sit on the curb and start crying. She was afraid if she started, she'd never stop.

The river levees had an even surface. She'd loved going through the Quarter in her youth. She went down the center of the street, where the pavement was flat, weaving her way through the neighborhood, and as she was passing Jackson Square, remembered that the police station was there. She stopped when she reached it, thought about going in, but couldn't remember the officer's name. It must be stress, so she kept going.

When she reached the Mississippi, she scaled up the grassy hill onto the top of the levee. It was always thrilling to see the river. Even in the pearly light of morning, the river was busy with barges and ships. She went in the direction of East New Orleans for seven miles, then turned around and went back.

She passed by Jackson Square again. Just as she went by the station, Detective Tom Ryan came down the steps. She happened to look up at the same time he did. He was taken aback by her appearance. She'd slept on her hair wet, so now it stood out from her head like a halo of red curlicues. In her T-shirt and shorts, her thinness was more obvious than in the filthy suit. She was as tall as he was. Maybe he hadn't noticed it last night, maybe she'd been stooped over from exhaustion, but he thought she was beautiful. The fact that she was covered in perspiration and that her clothes were soaking wet didn't seem to bother her. She appeared to be the most unselfconscious person he ever met.

"Well, hi there," he said.

She didn't reply, but walked over to him. She wasn't even out of breath.

"Just getting started?"

"I did the fifteen-mile circuit I used to do in high school. The birds woke me up at six so I got an early start."

Maybe it was a good thing she went without me; I'd be lucky to go a mile, he thought.

"Where are you headed to now?" He was hoping she would go for a cup of coffee, but something told him she was not going to be an easy one to get to know.

"Back to my friend's house. I have to get over to the funeral home this morning. I hope I hear something from court, too."

He had forgotten what her main purpose in coming to New Orleans was.

"If I can help you in anyway today, be sure to call me. I may be able to get some information for you if you aren't getting any answers." He'd make it about her, after all. "You have my card, right? My beeper number and cell phone are on it."

"Thanks. I better get going, and you need to get some sleep." She smiled and hit the pavement again.

He was intrigued, watching her as she ran from him. Her legs were so long, thin and muscular. He watched until she rounded the corner.

When she got home, Julia was waiting at the door with a towel and a glass of water. "You go first," Alexandra said, taking the water.

"What do you want to know?" Julia said, forgetting that she was the one who located the Rodríguez family.

"How'd you ever find Kathy Rodríguez?" Alexandra asked.

"I decided it would be easy to badger Dube while he was upset about your mother. I also threatened him. You know I have friends at the newspaper," Julia said. "But what are you going to do about the little ones?"

Alexandra had called Julia with updates while she was in Colleen's house, but she wanted details now.

"I'm their grandmother, so morally they are my responsibility. I'm supposed to wait for the court to call this morning. They were going to contact Dube to confirm that I'm who I said I am. We don't have a birth certificate or any proof that I'm the grandmother. They'll tell me what the judge decided and when I have to appear. The police officer who drove me home last night, Detective Ryan, gave me his card and said he would call for us if I didn't hear soon."

"But what about Elizabeth, I mean Colleen?" Julia asked. She was about to see the new Alexandra, the communicative woman who would repeat the story about going first to Kathy's house and receiving the shocking news and then making the decision to go to Colleen's house alone.

Alexandra thought how wisely young Jeff Gaugain had advised her when he said to let the legal system make its plans for her. Whatever they said, she would do. Unfortunately, it wouldn't tell her what she *wanted* to happen.

Julia asked the tough questions. "Do you want custody of the children?"

"I don't know," she said. Alexandra really didn't know. She wanted her daughter as a baby. As a mentally ill adult, she couldn't imagine dealing with her problems. She would, though, if asked. It's what a parent did. But want to? That was harder to decide. As far as wanting to be the guardian of her seven grandchildren, how could she not want them? She couldn't just take Nina. It would mean moving to a larger place, finding help, being unselfish. All she had ever done all of her adult life was think of herself, avoiding those things that had the power to effect her and accepting those things that were to her liking. She didn't know if she was mentally capable of raising children. Julia listened quietly and nodded her head to let her friend know she was listening. Alexandra was pouring it out for not being a conversationalist. She didn't ask Julia for her opinion.

Alexandra's cell phone rang at eight thirty. It was the registrar at Family Court reporting that the judge wanted to see her. Her heart sank. She asked Julia to come along, and if she froze due to stress, Julia could speak for her. They made an appointment for twelve thirty. Alexandra would have time to go to the funeral home first.

She would go to Dube's, too. Julia told her she should raise hell with Dube for the way he abandoned her. Alexandra hadn't dealt with it yet. She didn't see anything negative in her childhood except for the kidnapping of her baby. She knew intellectually that being beaten and neglected by her mother was a bad thing. She remembered a class she had in high school called The Psychology of the American Family. Alexandra was astonished that the picture painted in the book of an average family could be so completely unlike her own. Soon, her past would become an issue for her, giving her strength to do the unthinkable. But for now, she accepted that the only real way she'd get through this experience was to do it one moment at a time.

She and Julia had a lot of ground to cover before lunch. Julia was happy that Alexandra asked her to go with her to court. She always worried about Alexandra, who was frail and vulnerable, in spite of her stature and education. She couldn't see her living in Manhattan with seven kids, but maybe she'd be okay. She had lots of money, thanks to her hard work and Julia's brother, Robert, her investment advisor.

Alexandra lived like a monk. Robert called Loren weekly to find out why she wasn't at least spending money for groceries. He was part of a group of people who gathered informally on Alexandra's behalf. They included her lawyer, her boss, Peter Van Sant, and Robert's CPA. Julia made sure she was dressed appropriately. Peter saw to the hiring of the assistants who cared for her at home and work. The accountant paid her bills and doled out the cash on hand, which gathered dust as it grew in her apartment.

Chapter 18

The meeting with Dube, who wept when he saw her, saddened her. They didn't embrace, as you would expect a man and his daughter to do after so many years. What surprised Alexandra the most was how old Dube was. He hadn't changed for years, and then all of a sudden, he was an old man. She estimated that he was forty when she was born. That made him close to eighty now. Tess didn't join the reunion. Alexandra was surprised, since she'd heard from Julia that Tess never got over their separation as youngsters. They agreed that Catherine would be buried without any fanfare or wake. It made sense. It protected what little dignity she'd had in her tragic life. Alexandra was relieved when the meeting was over and she and Julia headed to court.

Alexandra was a law-abiding citizen. Since she didn't drive, she'd never even had a parking ticket. The world of courts and police were as foreign to her as space travel, and she had no idea what to expect. Having never even seen a television program about court (she didn't own a TV), she thought it might be like going to a doctor appointment, something she was very familiar with.

When they entered the courthouse, it was empty except for a man with an elderly woman and a young woman with two children who were leaving at the same time Julia and Alexandra arrived. It was Sunday, and only emergencies were processed on the weekend. She guessed her situation qualified as an emergency. Court took five minutes, tops. The receptionist led them into the judge's chamber, which was nothing more than a tiny, paneled office with a desk and three chairs. She told them to sit down, then left the room through a different door. Julia looked at Alexandra and smiled. They sat, two proper ladies, dressed appropriately for a day in town: ladies who lunch. A few minutes passed, and the judge came through the same door through which the receptionist had left.

He had food crumbs in his bushy mustache. Julia raised her gloved hand up to cover a smirk. She couldn't abide slovenliness. He shuffled some papers, didn't bother to introduce himself, and sat. He continued to read the papers. Eventually, he looked up at Julia and then Alexandra. She was secretly praying he wouldn't ask her what she wanted, but would just pronounce his judgment and they could get on with it. "Who's the grandmother?" he asked.

Alexandra raised her hand as if she was in school, saying, "I am."

"Are you prepared to take your grandchildren to live with you in New York City?" He pronounced it *New Yolk Ceety*. Alexandra tried to hide her reaction while Julia snickered, appalled.

She quickly said, "Yes."

He pounded the gavel once, saying, "Docket 459, Family Court of New Orleans gives full and permanent custody of Nina, Gloria, Sophia, Taylor, Morgan, Moira and Benjamin Rodríguez to Alexandra Donicka, resident of New Yolk Ceety, on this day of…"

It was over. Alexandra had custody of seven children she didn't know. They stood up. The judge leaned forward to shake their hands, Alexandra in a daze. *How did they figure out the children's names?*

He had one more thing to say to her, however. "Avoid your daughter like the plague." He looked at her over his glasses. "I advise you to get out of town as quickly as you can. She'll be incarcerated for thirty days. You have just that long." He swept his dirty, black gown around him and walked out of the room. The two women stood there looking at the door for a few moments, and then the receptionist came out. She had a large, manila envelope.

"I'll go with you to the Social Services office. The foster family that had your children will be bringing them back at two. A van will take you back to your daughter's house to gather their belongings." She could see the change in Alexandra's countenance. "Or not, you don't have to take anything from the house. It might make it harder on their mother to return home with everything still in place, however. Whatever we can do to reduce animosity sometimes is worth the effort."

They walked through a series of tunnels that connected the courthouse to the police station, where the Social Services office was. Alexandra was not prepared, and the temptation to fade into the background and allow Julia to do the work was strong. Julia was in her most aggressive stance, head held high, gloved hands at her sides.

They could hear the children before they saw them. Babies crying, the older ones babbling. They were led into another office with a high counter on which stacks of papers awaited Alexandra's signature. She was directed to sign paper after paper, an attorney at her side explaining what meant what and what she needed to have looked over by her own attorney.

"This group of papers gives you full and permanent custody of your seven grandchildren, with no visitation allowed by your daughter. There's no father named on any of the documents we have. The children have been in the system since birth, owing to repeated offenses by your daughter." He kept saying "your daughter" with a hint of derision. He pointed to a second grouping of papers.

"This group is to take with you. Read them when you are settled. I promise there are no surprises. You are eligible for federal aid. The courts want to keep children who have relatives out of the system. This is one way to do it. No frills, all the help you need, etc., etc. Any questions?"

Alexandra was beyond speech. Julia placed her hand protectively on her friend's arm and spoke up.

"Do you provide any kind of guidance? Someone who can advise us of what to do next? You can imagine we are unprepared for this. I want to help her do everything right."

Lovely Julia, always thinking of the other person, Alexandra thought. *She has every right to run as fast as she can from this mess.* She didn't know Julia was paying penance for not being a better neighbor thirty years ago to a young girl who was all alone.

"We do have an ombudsman. I'll give you some phone numbers." He turned and walked away. At the same time, Jeff Gaugain came out. He had a huge smile on his face.

"Come sit down. I bet you would like to know what to do next?" He waited for a response.

Both women shook their heads.

"Are you staying in a hotel?" he asked.

Alexandra shook her head.

Julia said, "She's staying with me." Not adding, *I live in a museum full of breakable treasures.*

"My advice is to go to a hotel," Jeff said. "Get a suite of rooms that's large enough for you to have your own space while you prepare to go back to New York. I'll set it up for you, if you'd like. There are nice hotels that are not too expensive, right here in The French Quarter. I'm going to give you the numbers of several agencies that provide immediate childcare so that you can tie up any loose ends you may have without dragging seven kids through town.

"I know the judge warned you about the mother. I disagree with him on that issue. If you go into the house without her approval, she can say you took her priceless jewel collection. What you *can* do is have a police officer go with you. Gather up anything of the children's. Throw it away if you want."

"Could I take the oldest child with me? She may be able to tell me about a favorite toy that we need to take," Alexandra said.

"That's a good idea. Whatever you do, do it now. Don't wait until tomorrow. Once word gets out into the community, who knows who will stop by the house while you're there. I want to avoid any hassles for you." Jeff stood up. "I have to go back now, but don't hesitate to call me." They shook hands again.

Alexandra turned to look down at Julia and whispered, "What the hell am I going to do?"

Chapter 19

The next hours were confusing and flew by like the wind. They took the children to the Riverwalk Hilton. It was a nice hotel with a pool so at least they might feel like they were going on vacation. The attorney had contacted a childcare agency, who sent two young women to the hotel within an hour. They took over so Alexandra could start making calls.

Peter Van Sant was first on her list, and she explained the entire story to him. "Your prize surgeon is turning out to be rather high maintenance," Alexandra said. "I'll need you to get a place for us to live that's big enough for seven kids."

"I'll do whatever I have to do to get you back here happy, and in one piece," he said.

His challenge would be to get the larger living quarters right away. She had the money to spare no expense, within reason. She wasn't Trump. Secondly, she needed him to hire full-time childcare and housekeeping. Peter had a bevy of informed people who he would put on this task right away.

Next, she called Eb Whitmore, her partner. He was shocked. *Alexandra, the surgical robot, a mother and a grandmother of seven? No fucking way*, he thought. He was supportive and loving out loud. "Whatever you need, my dear, I will get. Just get back here."

"Thanks, Eb," she said. "Can you handle things for a week?" She knew she was pushing it. How was she going to get seven kids to Manhattan, settled in school or with babysitters, in one week? She also asked him to spread the word around the OR and to tell Grace she would get a call, soon.

"I'll do whatever you want if it will get you back here," he repeated. "You know we can't manage without you."

She knew very well they could, but was touched by the sentiment.

Alexandra knew how lucky she was. Because of her position at the hospital and the money she had made, she had only to pick up the phone and her needs would be met. She had always been taken care of. What was it like for middle or lower income people who had problems dumped in their lap? Unthinkable.

After they got settled in, Julia and Nina went shopping for clothes, shoes, and diapers, bottles, formula, whatever the children might need.

Alexandra hesitantly pulled out a business card with the name Thomas Ryan on it. She would ask him to take her back to the house in the Ninth Ward. Nina had recited a list of things they might like to have, sparing her the pain of going back. The younger children each had a favorite item. The rest would be bagged up and placed at the curb for trash pick up. She had the document to prove this was standard operating procedure.

She punched in his number, and he answered on the first ring.

"Hi, sorry to bother you," she said, embarrassed.

"No, I'm glad you called," Tom said. "Did you hear from the court yet?"

"Yes," she replied. "I'm currently in a two-bedroom hotel suite on the river with seven kids, two babysitters and my friend."

"I take it this isn't a social call, then," he said, laughing.

"No, I actually have a huge favor to ask." Alexandra was losing her nerve, but thought, *This is for the children right now, and for Elizabeth in the end.*

"Okay, go ahead," he prompted.

"Would you consider going with me back to the Ninth Ward?" she asked. "I need to remove the children's belongings. Jeff Gaugain suggested I take an officer with me so I won't be accused of stealing anything."

"I'm free now. When do you want to go?" he asked.

"As soon as I order dinner from room service, I'm ready," she answered.

"Okay, I'm on my way," he replied.

Alexandra marveled at the conversation she'd been able to have without stumbling or long silences. She shook her head to clear her thoughts. There was no time in her schedule to introspect. Grabbing the room service menu off the desk in her room, she walked back into the sitting room, where everyone was congregating.

"What should we get for dinner?" she asked.

Amid the cheers and yelling, they chose hamburgers and spaghetti with salad. She'd never make the spaghetti mistake again; she found a piece of it stuck on the TV screen. Afterward she told the babysitters about her errand. They reassured her that everyone would be fine. Alexandra was impressed with their efficiency.

Tom came up to the rooms instead of calling for her at the registration desk. He was in his street clothes. She'd put on jeans and a T-shirt: serious work clothes. He was again surprised at how thin she was. *Those legs.* He tried not to think about her legs.

Amazed at the scene before him as seven children were stuffing spaghetti in their mouths, he whispered to her, "Feeding time at the zoo."

No one looked up to greet him or was even vaguely interested that she was leaving. It was good. She'd wondered if there might be a scene when she left, already taking possession of her family.

They left the hotel room together, Tom putting his hand on Alexandra's upper back when they walked through the elevator door. He had no way of knowing she hadn't like being touched until she found her daughter. When she'd grabbed her and held her the previous day, it was as though her need for space around her had diminished. When she felt his hand on her back, she thought it was a little nervy of him. *Is it commonplace for a stranger, a cop no less, to touch a woman like he had?* She made a mental note to ask Julia.

She felt relaxed around him, but wasn't ready to let her guard down. He was simply facilitating her goal of getting the children settled. They got to the squad car, and he opened the passenger-side front door for her.

"Shouldn't I sit in back?" she asked.

He shook his head. "Nope. In front, please. This is official police business."

Tom remembered the way to the house. They drove in silence for a few blocks before he asked her what it was like living in New York. No one had ever asked her.

"It's just a place where I live," she replied, confused.

Thinking he needed to be more specific, he asked her what she did when she wasn't working. Keeping it impersonal, she told him what it was like to be a runner in town. She knew the grid of the streets, which ones to avoid at which times of the day. Not confessing she liked the areas where homeless people stayed because she felt as though those places were where she fit in best. "It made me sad when the neighborhood around Tompkins Park started to gentrify. I don't like going through there now. When rent hikes threatened my favorite bodega in Chelsea, there was a possibility it might have to close.

"Across the street from my apartment is a coffee shop I go into every day. The owner always tries to engage me, but I ignore him," she said, looking at Tom. "I have a mental illness, you realize that, right?"

"I've been a cop a long time," he said. "If there's anything ill about you, I'd have picked up on it by now."

"Yeah, well, there's a lot you don't know," she said, thinking of her idiosyncrasies, like her relationship with food. She'd eaten nothing for almost two days. "Is there anyway you can stop somewhere so I can get something to eat? It just occurred to me that I haven't eaten much in a while."

She noticed his look and tried to ignore it. He took her hand, or attempted to take her hand. She didn't pull away exactly, but she didn't respond, either. "We can stop and have dinner if you want," he replied.

"No, I just need a piece of fruit," she answered.

He pulled into a parking space in front of a delicatessen and got out of the car before she could protest. He aimed his car key fob at the squad car, and the locks went down. It was dark out, and the neighborhood was not well lit. He came back shortly with a brown paper bag. He was grinning at her. He opened the door and slid in, tossing the bag to her.

"They have the best muffuletta in town," he said.

She peeked in the bag, and the smell of something tangy came out. It made her stomach growl.

"Eat up. I doubt you'll have an appetite after we get done with our errand."

"I didn't think of that," she said. "No wonder I haven't eaten."

He looked at her with raised eyebrows and nodded his head in agreement as he pulled out onto the street again.

"Right." He could tell by looking at her that food was not a big deal. He knew how hard it sometimes was to fix a meal when grabbing a bag of pretzels was easier.

He started talking about himself while she ate. "I'm curious about living in New York. I've always lived right here, born and raised in New Orleans. My parents are dead, unfortunately. First my mom three years ago, and then last year, my dad. I think about them every day.

"I live in the family house. It's about two blocks from where we saw each other at the station this morning. My sisters are both in Baton Rouge, so it was mine if I wanted it." He glanced over at her, and she was wrapping half the sandwich up in its waxed paper.

"*My* mother was insane," Alexandra answered. "She was once picked up for defecating on the sidewalk outside of the Commander's Palace. I'm sure you'll be able to find out more if you look up her name in your records."

"What about your father?" Tom asked softly, trying to hide his shock.

"He owns The Black Swan. My mother slit her wrists in the bathroom above the dining room there last week. Remember, my supposed reason for being here was for her funeral." Reciting her family history felt awful. Looking out the car window as they drove to the Ninth Ward, Alexandra had a revelation.

"Family histories are highly overrated. I did just fine without mine. As a matter of fact, I think it's amazing I was able to rise above their legacy." She looked over at Tom; his expression was unmistakable: a combination of admiration and desire. His interest made her skin crawl.

"Nothing is going to happen between us," she said smugly.

"Why do you say that?" Tom said, smiling.

"For one thing, it's totally inappropriate. *And* I live seven hundred miles from here," she said, looking out the window. She was not interested in any man, or any adult human, for that matter. Especially right now, after what she'd experienced in the past twenty-four hours. *I've been alone for so many years, and now with the children, there's no way. No way.*

"I'm not afraid to fly," Tom replied, trying to take her hand again.

"Look, I don't date, all right?" she said, exasperated, sure he was breaking some law by pressuring her like he was.

"Why? Are you a lesbian?" he asked.

She looked over at him with a frown. "That's none of your business," she answered. "Just drive, will you?"

Sensing she was angry, he stopped pushing her. He didn't give up her hand until they got to the house. It lay cold and still in his, like a dead thing. Now he was the nervous one, compelled to pursue a victim who was in distress. He was afraid he might get into trouble if he didn't slow it down.

The judge's warning was correct. There was a small crowd of people on the lawn of the house. They took off as the squad car pulled up when Tom turned on the lights and siren for one brief second. She quickly looked at him in surprise, giving out an involuntary laugh.

"Just for effect," he said. They walked up to the door, and Tom magically produced a key. "We took it from the kid

Saturday night." When he opened the door, the smell of filth hit them in the face.

"It seems my cleaning spree didn't do much good after all," she said, embarrassed that her daughter's slovenly lifestyle was public record. She'd wished she could have protected her.

"It's the trash, probably," he replied.

They avoided the kitchen and went back to the children's room. Alexandra got out Nina's list. She started searching for items. Any clothing appearing to be intact she stuffed in the bag. She gave Tom the task of picking up toys that looked safe and complete. She noticed there wasn't a book or crayon. The rest was thrown away.

Soon, ten large black plastic bags were stuffed with tattered clothing and broken toys. They piled up the trash bags in the living room, then went into the kitchen and retrieved the bags she'd filled two days ago. Tom emptied out what little stuff was in the refrigerator. Nothing would be edible in thirty days anyway. Then they piled the bags at the curb. Trash day was on Monday. Tom told the crowd gathering again that surveillance would be on the house and no one was to touch the trash.

"It's contaminated with bacteria that could make humans sick," he said.

Alexandra looked at him with suspicion.

"Well, it could be true."

They went back inside to scrub their hands. The crowd was creeping up again. Tom locked the house door, and they got into the squad car. When they took off, the car wasn't even out of sight when the crowd converged on the trash bags. Tom just laughed. "Hopeless."

"I don't think I want to take this stuff back to the hotel. What if it has cockroaches in it?" Alexandra said.

"Good point," Tom said. "Let's go to the Laundromat."

She nodded in agreement.

Alexandra thought it was generous of Tom to do laundry with her since she didn't have a clue how to use the machines. Watching his every move, she thought she could wash clothes now if she had to, in a pinch. Every toy was wiped down with a bleach wipe.

They carted the clean clothes up the elevator to the rooms, piling them on one of the beds. Alexandra introduced Tom to everyone. They distributed toys to the kids, who seemed more interested in Tom now that they'd finished eating. Ben wanted to know where his uniform and gun were if he was a police officer. He lifted up his jacket so the boy could see the gun. Ben squealed with delight. He was either advanced for his age, or going to be trouble.

Soon it was time for Tom to go to work. He said goodbye to everyone, reluctant to leave. Alexandra walked to the elevator with him, again thanking him for his kindness, trying to focus on how helpful he'd been and nothing else. The kids tried to follow, and the babysitters rounded them up. It would seem that this intrusion of children would be Alexandra's life from now on, and it made her happy.

"I'll probably go back to the city tomorrow. There are so many things to do. I have to find a bigger place to live, find schools and childcare. And I have to get back to work as soon as possible. It's making me nervous just thinking about it." She wasn't sure why she was telling him, except she felt she owed him an explanation.

"What can I do to help you?" he said, knowing she would probably refuse offers of help.

She thought of something he could do for her. "Would you keep tabs on my daughter?" She didn't say anything else, her feelings still in turmoil about what had happened, guilt too mild a word to describe it.

"Yes, I'd do it anyway as part of the investigation of child abuse," he said. "If you can, don't worry about her too much. As tempting as it might be to take the blame, she brought this on herself. I know Jerome Rodríguez, and you wouldn't find a better couple to raise your daughter."

Loyalty, defensiveness, and pride bubbled up in Alexandra, who also thought of her genetic contribution, but let it go. She didn't want to have that conversation while they waited for the elevator.

After he left, she went back to the suite to spend time with her grandchildren before they went to bed. Julia had bought a selection of children's books during her shopping expedition, and reading a bedtime story would become a routine. Alexandra's chosen job was to give the babies their baths. Afterward, she warmed up formula in new bottles by running hot water over them from the bathroom sink. One baby could hold her own bottle; the other needed to be fed.

While holding Moira, Alexandra leafed through the paperwork given her by the attorney. She found the birth certificates of the children among the papers. Nina was seven years old, Gloria six, Sophia five, Taylor four, Ben three, Morgan eleven months, and Moira three months. She wondered what happened between Ben and Morgan. Elizabeth could've had two more births in there. Alexandra didn't want to worry about Elizabeth. Tom gave her sound advice. She needed to focus on the children. She was so foolish about babies, thinking these two littlest ones were twins. Julia walked in just then.

"I actually thought these two were twins," Alexandra said.

"Aren't they?" Julia said, looking perplexed.

Alexandra gave a rare laugh out loud.

"Morgan is almost a year old, and Moira is an infant. If they haven't inherited anything horrible from my mother, they have a chance. I hope I don't accidentally kill anyone tonight. You know, like drop anyone on their heads."

"Oh, I think you'll do just fine," Julia said. "I'm the one we have to watch out for. *Unnatural*, I think is the term. You should have seen Nina look at me in the store. I had no idea what to buy. She exchanged a few glances with the saleslady. She said, 'Think clothes, food, shelter.' Only after we came away from the first store did I think of toys. We went into the bookstore. Books are better than toys." She'd bought games, stuffed animals and teaching toys.

After the babies were cared for, Alexandra put them in their cribs. It didn't occur to her that they may not want to sleep yet, but rather than disappoint her, they closed their eyes and dropped off. Alexandra looked in on the other children. She spoke briefly with Beth and Faye from the childcare agency. They said the children seemed well adjusted in spite of what they had been through over that weekend. Then Beth asked Alexandra if she would consider having her come to New York to help with the trip, and then stay on with the children as a nanny.

"I'm looking for a permanent position. It will be easier for me to stay in school if I have one job." She looked over at Faye. "It was actually Faye who thought this might be the right family for me. My major is child psychology."

Alexandra laughed. They could use a child psychology major in residence. "Would you want to come, too? We'll need two nannies," she asked Faye, but Faye shook her head.

"Thank you, but I can't," she replied, explaining that she had a husband and children in New Orleans. It was okay for her to be gone overnight occasionally on these emergency jobs, but she looked forward to going home tomorrow afternoon. Beth was single. She joined the agency initially so she could have some flexibility, but found after a while that it might be easier to find a permanent job.

If Beth could travel with the children, it would eliminate the worry Alexandra had about how she would manage on the plane. She didn't want to ask Julia to come on the trip, but was considering it, when Julia herself spoke up.

"Pardon me for barging in, but I will go with you on the plane. I won't take no for an answer." She was looking awfully fetching in a bright red terry cloth bathrobe, filing her nails. Alexandra let that be the end of the conversation.

"If everyone will forgive me, I have some phone calls to make before it gets too late." Alexandra took her phone and went to a small sitting room that adjoined her room. She looked up her assistant's phone number and punched it in. Then she texted, *May, I need,* and she counted out loud, *ten plane tickets to Kennedy tomorrow, from New Orleans. If it is possible, in the late afternoon, but not too late. Not the morning. Two tickets will be for babies under a year, if that makes a difference. They should have their own seats. Ask Grace for details. Thanks for everything you do for me. Alexandra.*

She thought that ten tickets should cost a small fortune. These rooms cost a fortune, too. She, who never gave a thought to money, was suddenly worried about it because she had no idea what she had. The next move would be to contact her accountant and find out. Then she punched in Grace's number, hoping to catch her before May called.

Grace picked up on the first ring, seeing Alexandra's number on her caller ID. "Peter said to wait for your call. What happened?"

Alexandra repeated her story, keeping to the facts. *Isn't the bare minimum bad enough? I don't need to embellish with the ugly details.*

"I am a terrible friend," Grace replied when Alexandra stopped long enough to take a breath. "All of these years and I had no idea what you were going through, how you were missing your daughter."

Alexandra never considered Grace a *friend*; she was a loyal colleague who was paid to work with her, but a friend? When she had a chance, she'd think more about it.

"I've been too numb to relate any of this. The only reason I'm able to do so now is that I need everyone's help. It's against my nature to fraternize; you know that better than anyone does. Even Eb offered to help," Alexandra confided with a chuckle. "Anyway, be prepared to repeat the story all you want. I just texted May to get ten tickets home. And now I have to call Loren, who is going to hate all of this chaos."

Before they said goodbye, Alexandra said she'd see her at work toward the end of the week. Grace said she'd send Monday's schedule. After they hung up, Alexandra could feel the anxiety creeping in. How could she be thinking of going back to work already? Her body was rebelling by her stomach churning. In the recent past, she'd dealt with such issues by going out to run. But tonight it didn't even cross her mind. The light in Julia's room was shining under the door. She knocked and asked if she'd like anything from room service, the half sandwich she'd eaten earlier with Tom a distant memory. They ordered a late night snack.

Right before midnight, Alexandra's cell beeped twice, the last text of the night. It was May, who'd booked ten seats on American Airlines Flight 198 to Kennedy leaving at five. A limo would pick them up at two, just in case traffic was bad. Cart service would take them to the gate. Explaining the story to the airlines got a great deal: ten tickets for $3,000, about half the usual price.

Moira woke up just as Alexandra was going to bed. A bottle ready in the refrigerator just needed warming up. She fed the tiny baby, cradling her in her arms. The act brought memories flooding back of those first hours in the shack with her new baby. She remembered holding Elizabeth. Tears rose, but she fought them back. She had to be strong now for these babies. She mustn't allow thoughts of the daughter she was leaving behind destroy her.

At the very moment Alexandra was struggling with her emotions, an apparition of a woman was clenching her fists and screaming through the bars of her hospital room/jail cell.

"Fucking bitch, leaving me to rot in this goddamned hole!"

"Knock it off, Rodríguez!" said Rhonda, the prison guard. The new prisoner was making noise and disrupting the peace of the ward. Rhonda had a headache from listening to the continuous complaining and yelling. If a prisoner had the energy to yell like this, she was strong enough to be transferred in with the regular population.

Ignoring the guard, there were more screams, this time without words. It was the sound of a woman in pain, frustration and livid anger, added to withdrawal from various illegal substances. Her blood and urine contained high levels of Vicodan, methamphetamine, cocaine and marijuana. When she awoke from the stupor Alexandra had left her in, her first question was, "What jail is this?" She didn't recognize the medical unit at the old New Orleans prison. It was set up the same as a jail with individual cells, but the lighting was better, and there was a video camera perched up high out of reach, recording the movements of the patient. Her attorney, Manny Rivola, was waiting to talk to her. He was an old friend of

Jerome, a tired-looking, frail man in his sixties, who dreaded the encounter with his client. The minute she saw him, she started to yell at him.

"Get me outta here! What are you doing? Get me outta here!" She repeated the phrases over and over again.

Manny said, "I'm leaving right now unless you stop yelling. You won't know what's going on unless you shut up right this minute." Manny secretly detested Colleen Rodríguez, only tolerating her for the sake of her father. He thought she was a spoiled, overindulged bitch whose current situation was just the tip of the iceberg. He didn't know if he had the skills to get her out of the mess she'd gotten herself into. She wasn't aware that she no longer had custody of her children. They were on their way to New York City with a woman who showed up when his client was at her very worst. If not the New York doctor, it would have been the state of Louisiana who took them away. He had seen the documentation on the case, and it was reprehensible what a friend said she had planned for her children. There were also rumors that she might have murdered a male baby she had given birth to. He didn't know what evidence there was, but just the murmuring was enough. He knew he might have to bow out of her defense.

"Are you ready to talk to me quietly?" Manny asked. She was pouting, and he thought she was struggling not to stomp her foot.

"Yes. But I don't have anything to say because I don't know what the hell happened!" She looked awful, smelled worse. She had on pale yellow scrubs. There was something dried on the front of the top that he didn't even want to think about. He would certainly tell the guard that she needed a bath.

He pulled a chair up to her cell. He knew it was dangerous to sit so closely to her, but didn't want to tell her what he had to say over a phone with glass between them.

"You have to promise me that you won't spit at me or try to throw anything at me, Colleen," Manny said.

"Okay, I promise. But why would I do that?" She just couldn't let him have the last word.

"First of all, sit down."

She pulled a chair around and sat.

"The bad news is that your children have been removed from your home, permanently. You had high levels of illegal drugs in your system when you were admitted. Your children were in your home with a woman who claims to be your mother. She couldn't leave them alone with you unconscious. There's an allegation that someone came into your home and raped Nina. Do you have any knowledge of that?"

"She was treated for an infection," Colleen said. "That's all I know."

"Once you are stable enough, you will be transferred to the state facility in Baton Rouge for thirty days," Manny said.

Colleen sat in the chair, speechless, looking at him. She was afraid that if she moved, she would explode. She wished she had a gun. She'd kill him first, then that fat-ass guard. She took a deep breath, already planning what her next move would be.

"Okay, so what's next? Are you going to arrange bail?" she asked, trying to compose herself.

"What's next is that the police are saying that they have uncovered some evidence that you might have murdered a baby boy. What evidence could they have against you?" Manny was playing possum.

"I don't know what the hell they're talking about! It's bullshit," Colleen said, fear creeping in. Evidence? She needed girls to fulfill her goals, not boys. But no one knew, no one saw. It was bullshit. She would stick to that, and if they had evidence, let them charge her with murder.

"Colleen, if you aren't completely honest with me, I can't help you, I can't defend you. Think about that, okay?" Manny stood up to leave.

"Wait. Where are my kids? Will I be able to see them?" she asked.

"They're on their way to New York City with your biological mother." He'd wondered if she would even ask about the children.

She flew up from the chair and started screaming again. "I knew that bitch put me here, but I didn't know she took my kids. God damn it, Manny, get them back! How do we know she's even related to me? I want my kids back!" she screamed.

He was tempted to walk away. He stood up.

"God damn it, don't leave, Manny. Get my kids back!" Her face was flushed, making the acne and scratches stand out vividly. Manny couldn't stand to look at her.

"Your children are no longer yours, Colleen. You got high one too many times. It was your responsibility to stay drug free, you knew that," he said.

"That's bullshit. Those are my kids," she screamed. "They're mine!" She flung herself around the cell, throwing her pillow and toilet articles. That was all it took for Manny. He got up and walked away. The guard shook her head and opened the door for him. All the while Colleen was yelling as loudly as she could.

"Get back here, Manny. Don't leave! Don't leave me here!"

To the guard, he said, "Sorry," and walked out of the jail.

Chapter 20

Alexandra woke up at five and tiptoed into the bathroom to dress, then into the children's room to tell Beth she was going out for about an hour. When she got back, the little ones were beginning to stir. She decided to allow the morning to unfold naturally. They would have to leave for the airport after lunch. Alexandra felt she had to say goodbye to Elizabeth before she left New Orleans, no matter how painful it would be.

Julia was alarmed when she told her. "I wonder if you shouldn't contact a lawyer first. So much happened that was out of your control. What do you think?"

"I'm not sure," Alexandra replied. She really *wasn't* sure. But she initiated contact with her daughter, and it resulted in seven children being removed from their mother's care and placed into her own *permanent* care. If Elizabeth got clean, she would deserve to see her children again. She was prepared for her daughter's wrath, whatever happened.

"I'm going. I have to do it." She had made up her mind. Alexandra left the hotel to walk to the prison.

When she arrived, the guard told her she would have to wait to see Colleen as her attorney was with her, and only one visitor was allowed. Alexandra sat down in a wooden chair that reminded her of the old chairs in her classroom at the high school. They were hard and straight backed. No one would fall asleep in these chairs. Soon a tired-looking gentleman walked through the door. He came right up to Alexandra.

"Dr. Donicka, I'm Manny Rivola, Colleen Rodríguez' attorney." He offered a hand to Alexandra, and she took it. He sat down next to her.

"You don't have to say anything to me if you don't want to. I know my client will contest the custody decision. And as much as I hate to say it, I will probably defend her at the hearing. Her father is an old friend of mine. She deserves a hearing so she can tell her side of the story. Right now, it doesn't look good because of her drug abuse. But I'm not sure this thing was done fairly or within the confines of the law, although I am sure the officers involved will disagree." He dug a white, ironed hankie out of his suit pocket and wiped his forehead off. He looked at Alexandra.

She hesitated for a long moment, not sure what to reply to this.

"I'm just following what the court dictates, Mr. Rivola. This is not what I intended would happen when I came to meet Colleen. I didn't even know she had children," she said.

"How did you find her?" he asked.

"My father told me who had adopted her, and I just followed that lead. My mother took her away without my consent. But I have wanted to find her all of my life. My mother died last week, and this was my first chance. I had no idea it would happen so quickly. To make matters worse, I barely exchanged two sentences with her when she asked for money and left. I was alone with the children for six hours, maybe more."

"What happened when she got home?" Manny asked.

"When she returned home, she immediately went to the couch and crashed. I wasn't sure if she was dead or just overdosed. I thought of leaving, but didn't want to leave the children alone. The oldest child told me a friend of Colleen's had raped her. That was when I decided to call the police. I wanted her to get medical care." She was so confused that night. Her daughter had totally manipulated her.

He took her hand again. He sincerely felt sorry for her. "You have your hands full. But something tells me you'll manage just fine," he said. They stood up together. He looked up at her, a little shocked at how tall she was. They smiled simultaneously.

"I want to see her before we leave today." She was stating a fact, not asking permission.

He shook his head. "Oh, I don't think I would do that if I were you. She is in a miserable state right now. Why not wait until she detoxes and come back. It should be okay to see her in another week or two." He could see the disappointment on her face. "Doctor, truly she won't care if you're sorry for what happened. She wouldn't care if you were God come down to absolve her from her sins. She's like a trapped beast in there. She just gave me hell and chased me away from her cell."

"How can I leave for New York with her children and not see her? I feel overwhelmingly that she is going to hold this against me." Those words would haunt her later on.

They said goodbye, and she left the jail without seeing Elizabeth. She hurried past the police headquarters, hoping she wouldn't run into Tom Ryan again.

The children were ready to go by the time she made it back to the hotel, quietly entertaining themselves, like the first time she was with them. It was clear they liked order, and Alexandra would see to it that their new life was orderly. The little boy, Ben, ran up to her and wrapped his arms around her legs, burying his face in her jeans. She reached down and patted his head. He lifted his arms up to her.

Everything was packed and the rooms given last minute once-overs by Julia. Alexandra was becoming quieter by the moment, holding Ben on her hip. Julia was afraid this would be too much for her, but what were they to do? She asked her if she was all right.

"What choice do I have? Right about now I would like to retreat into the old Alexandra." But she smiled. "One foot in front of the other. One of my strengths."

They nodded in agreement. Alexandra counted heads, and they left the room. The lobby was full of people, and the women with their bevy of children drew smiles. Alexandra looked at the floor as she walked out of the hotel. Their gathering was the result of tragedy and would amount to brutal heartache for someone else. She didn't feel like any attention they drew would be good for their karma. *Deep breath, kiddo,* she thought to herself. *Don't go nuts on everyone now.*

The limo pulled up right at the stroke of two, just as May told her it would. They piled in, the driver helping the porter with their many bags. Julia pulled more dollar bills out of her purse for tips. Faye was going to the airport to help and then back to her own home. Each of them had a baby, and Alexandra was still carrying Ben. The little girls looked so sweet in their new clothes. Nina reminded Alexandra of herself at that age. Very tall and proper. Still innocent. She hoped she would be able to give them all love. She felt emotion for them. She would have to move fast to figure it all out.

They were rushed through security and helped with boarding the plane. Alexandra never had a chance to feel frightened because she was so worried about the safety and well-being of her grandchildren. The focus was no longer introspective.

When the flight was over and the plane had landed safely, they were allowed to stay on the plane until the crowds had rushed off. The carts were waiting to take them to the baggage claim. Porters helped retrieve their baggage, and the limo was waiting.

It was cold out after the sweltering heat of New Orleans, but they made a fast exodus from the airport into the limo, and no one suffered. The city skyline mesmerized the older children. Alexandra felt anxiety bubbling up inside of her. She told Julia that she didn't know if there was any food in the house or where they would sleep. In seconds, during the ride to Chelsea, Alexandra solved all her problems with one idea, get a hotel again. She asked the limo driver if he could help them out. He picked up his cell phone and made a call to his dispatcher, who in turn made another call and fixed them up at the Meridian Hotel in Madison Square, about six blocks from her apartment. They had a large efficiency suite available. Alexandra immediately relaxed, and Julia praised her quick thinking.

Once everyone was settled in and dinner was ordered, she would go to her apartment and see what could be done. What was she thinking, bringing seven kids to Manhattan? She thanked Julia, who was ready to call it a night. She put on her sneakers, gave Beth her itinerary, and ran out the door.

When she got to Eighth Avenue, the familiar buildings, even the streetlights she knew, helped her to relax. She was so glad to be home. What a horrible weekend. She didn't get a chance to think about her dead mother. She knew she'd eventually have to face her anguish about her daughter.

She'd remembered to take her keys, hanging them around her neck on the cord. She let herself into the building, noticing that the lights were on in her apartment. She unlocked the door and found her entourage, Peter Van Sant, Grace, May and Loren. They looked shocked at first, and then when the confusion died down and Alexandra had a chance to tell them they were in a hotel, they agreed it was a brilliant idea. They could see the change in her. She addressed May while it was fresh in her mind.

"Everything, from the moment we left the hotel in New Orleans, was perfect. Just as you said, the limos arrived, the carts were there, and I just had to stand with a baby on each hip. I cannot thank you enough."

"If you think what I did was so great, wait till you see what Loren and Grace did," May said.

Alexandra looked on as the flurry began. First, they pulled her into her tiny kitchen to see the cupboards and fridge well-stocked with things that tykes eat, as Peter referred to the children. Then she noticed, for the first time, furniture. Chairs and tables, low for children, and a higher set, for eating. They dragged her into the spare bedroom, where two sets of bunk beds, perfect for the girls, were set up. In her bedroom were two cribs and a small youth bed for Ben. The sofa made into a bed for the babysitter, Beth. They thought of everyone, except for Julia, who was best off staying in a hotel anyway.

Loren knew about Beth, but felt they needed a second person to come in during the day. Her cousin Maria was available full time. She had her green card and spoke English. Her specialty was cooking, but she would gladly do housekeeping and help with baby care. The apartment was too small to accommodate more than one additional caregiver; once she had a larger space, they'd hire another person.

Peter discovered that the apartment above Alexandra's, an updated three bedroom, was for sale. With the addition of an inside stairwell, it would make a great two-story flat. They could remove the galley kitchen in the lower level or leave it. Whatever she wanted they could do. Alexandra felt that it was just too convenient, that apartment above hers. Paranoia was creeping in. Right now, all she wanted was to get back to the hotel. She'd stay focused on the tasks she needed to complete: moving her new family to the tiny apartment and finding a school for the girls and a nursery school for Ben. Nina was bright, but she would have a tough time catching up.

Alexandra was used to others controlling her and making decisions on her behalf. It would work in her favor now that she was so busy. She turned to Peter. "Would you find someone to handle the purchase of the flat? And deal with the staircase? I can't focus on it."

He agreed, saying he'd place his entire resources at her disposal if it meant keeping her at the medical center.

"I appreciate everything you have done. There is no way in the world I could have ever have managed this without you all. But I have to get back to the hotel now," she said. As she walked down the staircase, she could hear their voices whispering, like they did when she was working.

One last quick run and she would be renewed. She arrived at the Meridian, and when she stepped off the elevator, there was a huge pile of dishes on a serving tray outside of their room. Room service hadn't let her down. Using her key, she quietly entered their suite. Julia must have gone to bed. Beth was lying in bed on top of the spread with her arms crossed behind her head. Five children in various sizes were sitting cross-legged on a sheet spread on the carpet. All of them were watching an old classic children's movie. There wasn't a peep to be heard. Alexandra made a mental note to buy the book. It would be a good place to start reading to them.

No one heard her come in, so she tiptoed into the bathroom and closed the door. She'd take a shower and get ready for bed. She grabbed a piece of hotel stationary and a pen. Sitting on the closed toilet seat, she made a list of what she had to do the next day. She knew that needs would pop up, and she would address them as they did. She couldn't even begin to anticipate what the children would need for school. But first she had to get them enrolled. There was a private school around the block. It would be less traumatic if they could go to school in the neighborhood. She had no idea what it would take to get them in, but hoped it would just be money. They needed clothes, too. Loren might agree to shop for them. Wishing she could go out and run again, she got into bed. It would be a long night.

The next morning, Alexandra had her run. When she got back to the hotel, Nina and Gloria were up, snooping around the suite.

"Good morning," Alexandra whispered as she closed the door behind her. "What's going on?"

"Did you go out to run?" Nina asked, learning the rhythm of her new life.

"I did," Alexandra said. "Did you have a good night?"

They nodded their heads.

"Is this where you live?" Gloria asked.

Nina swatted her arm. "No, silly, this is the hotel."

"But where do you live, Alexandra?" Gloria asked. She wasn't going to let her older sister stop her from getting her questions answered.

Alexandra was worried about Gloria. She had a look about her eyes. She also had a very short attention span. Alexandra was concerned about fetal alcohol syndrome. It was something that would be investigated soon.

"I live about six blocks from here," Alexandra answered. "But it's a small apartment, and I was afraid you would feel crowded there. I never had children in my house. A friend bought beds, sheets and pillows for you."

"Cribs, too?" Taylor asked.

"Yes, my dear, cribs too." Alexandra was starting to feel that old anxiety welling up, just as the dreaded question was asked.

"Where's my mom?"

She decided she had to be truthful about everything. She was unable to contrive, a weakness for sure when dealing with children.

"She was taken to the medical center for a few weeks until she gets better." Keep it basic and simple.

"Was she sick?" Taylor asked.

Alexandra nodded her head.

"When will she come home?" Sophia asked.

"In about a month. I know she wouldn't want you to worry, though," Alexandra said, lying. She wanted to change the subject.

"Let's get breakfast from room service, and then we can think about going to our new home!" She turned her back to find the menu, asking herself once again what in hell she thought she was doing.

Chapter 21

Manhattan is, to those who love it, all that is required to live happily on Earth. A place to store a few belongings, a bed to rest your body, and the rest of the city is your home. Alexandra unconsciously lived that kind of life. She found everything she needed in the city. No part of town frightened her. Where others wouldn't tread after dark, Alexandra fearlessly ran. Her patients included indigents found half dead on the city streets and kings from foreign lands who came to America to have her cut into their brains. Her reputation preceded her since her lab days in New Orleans, when a PhD in Biology once saw her, a high school student, dissect the brain of a chimpanzee and asked if she was a brain surgeon.

Every area of her being that had been devoid of substance—her inability to fully communicate with people, her dearth of social skills, her absence of common sense—was funneled into that gift, the treasure that was her fingers holding a scalpel. She had a magical sense that allowed her to see past bone and dura. She could visualize structures within the skull of her patients, enabling her to bypass vital tissues and go right to the diseased parts. She was quick and sure, humble and kind.

Now, she had to tap into an area of her intellect thus far untouched, and she was concerned it would encroach upon her gift. She had to share her life. She had to develop common sense to care for her grandchildren. She thought about it more and more as the hours passed. *Her children.* She would have a life because of the children.

Her life was changed, and it changed her. She was a little frightened how it would manifest itself. Other surgeons had wives or husbands and children, houses on the island, boats and motorhomes, fishing trips, collections. She had an empty apartment. She didn't even own a television. These thoughts monopolized her till the wee hours of the morning.

When it was late enough to get up and get moving, she'd let the children sleep in and have a leisurely breakfast without her. She would go for a run and then come back and dress for the school searches. She decided to cold call. She couldn't stand talking on the phone.

It took an act of her will to go back to the apartment, not because she was dreading it, but because she loved being out on the street after her weeklong absence. Running in Manhattan was different from running in the French Quarter, like doing roadwork instead of cross-country. Two different beasts. But she wasn't just about Alexandra anymore, so she squelched the desire to keep going and returned to the apartment.

Loren was dropping off Alexandra's cleaning. She introduced herself to Beth and Julia, then the four older girls. After meeting the children, Loren was moved after having criticized Alexandra to her family and friends for being one of the most self-absorbed women she had ever known. She was worried that a woman who couldn't dress herself properly was suddenly guardian to seven kids. Seeing them together, she decided to change her attitude and be supportive, not critical. Alexandra would need all the help Loren had to give.

Already she could see a subtle change in Alexandra, who didn't look at the floor when talking, and was touching another human being without latex gloves. Loren had provided large, covered containers for each child's belongings. Until they had space for dressers and armoires, the containers would have to do. She would call her cousin Maria to come and start work now. The children were excited having their own, new belongings. Julia set out writing their names in large, block letters on the containers. The girls saw their names in writing for the first time. Julia sat on the floor in her Chanel suit and began the first of many lessons in the alphabet with four little girls.

Alexandra let Beth decide how to organize the baby's things while she got ready for her day finding appropriate schools for her grandchildren. She picked up files, said good-bye, and started out.

Two short blocks from her house was a large, Victorian brownstone, encircled by elaborate wrought-iron fencing. There was a large play area in back with beautiful swings and slides. It housed a privately run school, known for its stringent admission standards and for its snobbery, issues Alexandra wasn't aware of. The headmistress's son had been a patient of hers three years before when diagnosed with a cancerous tumor close to his brain stem. She successfully removed his tumor with no residual damage. The family was grateful; the mother beside herself with praise for the doctor who'd saved her son's life. Alexandra would use the gratitude to gain her grandchildren's admittance to the school.

She entered the front yard, file folder under her arm. Going up the steps of the building, she had déjà vu; over thirty years before she'd walked up the steps of an old Victorian building that housed her elementary school in New Orleans and began the odyssey of education. Of all the horrors her grandchildren had encountered, the absence of learning would have the greatest impact if not corrected right away. Forgetting her pride, awkwardly, she would beg her patient's mother for the good of her grandchildren. She would recreate their life, and it would start here, at this school, close to home.

The first hurdle she encountered was the receptionist. She wasn't going to budge. Enrollment for spring was closed. Alexandra explained that she needed enrollment for this week.

"We never allow children to start in the middle of a semester," she said firmly.

"But what about children who move to the city in the middle of a term?" Alexandra asked.

"Our parents would never move their children in the middle of a semester," she replied.

"Please, I must speak with the headmistress. I know if you tell her I'm here, she'll see me. Just tell her Dr. Donicka is here. I took care of someone she knows." Alexandra had all day to plead and was completely honest and not trying to be disrespectful. But she would get her grandchildren enrolled.

"Wait here," she said. The receptionist rose and walked through a door, shutting it quietly behind her.

Alexandra heard a raised voice. The door was thrown back open, and a stylish, older woman, the mother of her patient, came rushing through.

"Dr. Donicka! Oh my goodness, I can't believe you stopped by," she said. She came at Alexandra and threw her arms around her, hugging her. Alexandra hid her cringe. "To what do I owe the pleasure?" She led Alexandra into her office, telling the receptionist to hold calls, no interruptions, please.

"Sit down, sit down! Will you have tea with me?"

Alexandra nodded while Mrs. Yardley buzzed somewhere in the school and asked for tea to be served.

"I won't take up your time with details. I brought my seven grandchildren home with me last night, from New Orleans. Three of them are school age. They have never been to school, but they appear intelligent. Last night, we read together, and they are sponges. You know I live here in the neighborhood. I want them to go to your school," she said.

"I'd be happy to have your grandchildren here, Doctor." She took a sip of tea, pondering for a moment. "If they haven't been in school yet, perhaps we can set up a private classroom for them, bring them up to level, and then mainstream them into the regular classroom. How does that sound?"

Alexandra took a sip of tea, not sure of her voice. Then she nodded her head.

Mrs. Yardley patted her knee. "This will be easy, my dear. I'll give you some forms to fill out. The children will have to have immunizations. We will bypass admission testing until right before they start in the regular classroom."

Alexandra thought of Gloria's possible problems but didn't mention it. They might be her imagination, she who had little experience with children.

They sipped tea for a few moments. Alexandra asked Mrs. Yardley for referrals for a nursery school for the younger children.

"I'll take the littler ones, too. We have a special nursery school slash daycare that runs as long as the average work hours," she said.

Beth would have just the two babies, after all.

They stood up and shook hands, Alexandra thanking Mrs. Yardley for her help and turning to the door before she tried to hug her again.

The receptionist had a pile of forms and information packets for her to take home. It included a financial package, which Alexandra would pass right on to her accountant. She thanked her and left the building. It was cold and drizzly when she got outside. She walk-ran the two blocks home. Quietly letting herself in, she observed her family peacefully sitting around Julia as she read them *Robin Hood*, one of the books she'd picked up in New Orleans. Ben was sitting right next to her, eyes round, listening to every word. Alexandra decided then she would not buy a TV right away.

She went into her bedroom, placing the papers from the school on her desk. She would deal with that later today. She called Peter first. Without saying hello, she launched right in. The old Alexandra was back.

"I need a pediatrician," she said.

"James Fellows," he answered. "I'll call him for you. What do you think about the apartment?"

"Good. Do it," she said.

"I'll call the realtor back right away, then. Alexandra?" But she had hung up.

Chapter 22

Alexandra leafed through the file the court had given her. Among the papers, she found eight birth certificates. One of them was a post-birth recorded certificate for Colleen Carol Rodríguez. It listed her parents as Kathy and Jerome. Alexandra didn't care about the omission of her name. But seeing the certificate caused a physical response that sickened her. She had taken her daughter's children without any explanation and left her in jail. She went to the stool by the window and sat down, waiting for the sensation to leave her body. Julia came to the door of her room and tapped.

"Come in," she said softly.

Julia noted her pale skin and the line of perspiration across her upper lip. Something unpleasant was going on.

"Are you okay?" she asked, going to her friend and placing her hand on the bony shoulder.

"I think I need to go back to New Orleans," Alexandra answered.

"Well, before you do that, come with us for a walk. I think fresh air will do the children good, and I'm certain it will do me some good," Julia said.

Alexandra glanced at her. "Are *you* okay?"

"Just come with us," she said.

Alexandra got off the stool and followed Julia out into the living room. The girls were excited, giggling and pushing each other. Alexandra noted that for having such a shitty life, they were really pretty well adjusted. She would have to delve into their lives more, find out how they spent their days, who they were with most of the time. Maybe Colleen had a friend that acted as babysitter who was kind and motherly. As they were buttoning up coats and pulling new mittens over little hands, Maria and Beth were stone-faced and silent. Since this was Alexandra's usual conduct, she didn't notice the behavior in others right away.

They had two strollers, a piggyback twin and a single. The older girls were hanging on to Alexandra, competing for her attention as she told them about the new school they would be going to. They walked to Twenty-Ninth Street. Chelsea Park had great swings, and chances were that few children would be there because it was a school day. They would have the whole place to themselves. When the swings came into view, the screams and excitement from the girls thrilled Alexandra. She grabbed their hands and yelled, "Hold on to each other," and they ran toward the swings. Everyone grabbed one. The babies were sound asleep in their strollers. Alexandra happened to look over at Julia and could see that something was wrong.

"What's going on?" she asked.

Julia motioned for her to come closer so she could whisper to her. "We got an earful while you were gone this morning. Evidently, the mother was videotaping the children," she paused, clearly appalled.

"Doing…oh no," Alexandra concluded, and Julia looked at her with a grim expression and nodded her head. Alexandra looked away, her brain spinning as the thoughts of her own experiences flooded her memory. Now this? Her daughter, the perpetrator?

"It sounds to me like she had them do it on a regular basis, the mother instructing the children, so she must have been selling the tapes," Julia continued. "I wrote down what was said, and now I want to call that young man who was so kind from the police department." She looked over at Alexandra and decided she'd said enough. The color had drained from her face so that she looked like a gray skeleton. She was pushing the swings and just standing, looking from child to child, from Beth, to Julia, to Maria. Beth said something to Julia, and she nodded her head. *So the others had heard, too.*

Julia had referred to "the mother." Elizabeth. No one Alexandra knew. Her flesh and blood, but only that. Not the recipient of her love, her influence, her guidance. She remembered the toothless grin of her baby, the tiny baby lying in the childish, thin arms. She sang to her and loved her for three brief months, obviously not long enough to make a difference. How did it all happen? Why? What would the cosmic benefit be? What was Elizabeth's purpose on Earth? Was it to have seven children to abuse and neglect? The pain was growing underneath her heart. Only hours before she was considering flying to New Orleans, and now she didn't think she had the stomach for a meeting with her daughter again. The joy of the day, the success of getting the children in school, was destroyed. Alexandra was relieved when the children had enough swinging and started asking for food.

They walked back toward the apartment slowly, the girls running ahead, Beth yelling for them to stop and wait when they got too far up the street. The adults stood two abreast, walking side by side, talking quietly about what was told that day, horrified, and dreading what would be the outcome. Julia was going to make the call, Beth getting on the extension. Alexandra didn't hear it, so she would be exonerated from this mess.

They stopped at a corner hot dog place and got food. As they ate, Beth said, "I'm not a superstitious person, but I think that there is something very spiritual going on here. You lost a kid, but got seven in return."

Alexandra bit her tongue; what Beth had just said was the complete opposite of what Alexandra was thinking.

"Isn't that akin to if you kill a fly, hundreds of his friends and family return for the body?" Julia said in her thickest fraudulent southern accent. She wasn't in the mood for any melancholy crap. "Let's get this call over with," she said, motioning to move toward home.

The children took their food and cups of juice with them, spilling on the pavement as they walked.

They walked in silence as thoughts of her new responsibilities swirled around Alexandra's brain. She needed to get a child psychologist on board, make dental appointments for them all, and ask for mercy from her business partner. She might be able to make up OR time, but there was no way she could see patients on a regular basis. That stress would exacerbate her lunacy to its fullest. She was feeling smothered again, but fought it down. She couldn't run away anymore.

As soon as they got home and the children settled with Maria, Julia signaled to Beth to pick up the extension as she dragged Alexandra into her bedroom, closing the door behind them.

"I want you to hear what's said." She dialed the New Orleans police department number and asked for Detective Ryan. They had forgotten that he worked the night shift and wouldn't be in until after six. Since the children weren't in any danger now, they decided to wait to talk to him directly, rather than another officer. Then, Alexandra remembered that she had his business card with his private number. She dug through her bag and produced the card. Julia gave her the phone even though Alexandra really didn't need to be involved yet. She dialed the number, and he answered on the first ring.

"Tom? This is Alexandra Donicka. Yes, thank you, our flight was fine. Well, the reason I'm calling is that my granddaughters revealed a disturbing account to my friend Julia. We thought of you right away. Could I put her on the line? No, I didn't hear it."

She handed the phone over to Julia. The next minutes were torture for Alexandra. The details were worse than she could have imagined. The littlest of the girls had knowledge they wouldn't have unless they'd been exposed to unsavory activity. How would they ever heal from such horrific experiences? Alexandra knew from her own experience that it was extremely difficult. The amazing fact was that they appeared so normal. She remembered the story Kathy told of Elizabeth's behavior as a toddler. Could such actions be inherent? It hardly seemed possible.

Julia said goodbye and tried to hand the phone over to Alexandra, who looked confused and backed up with her hands up, shaking her head. She did *not* want to talk to him.

"He wants to talk to you," Julia whispered, pushing the phone at her. She took the phone.

"Yes," she said. She wasn't in the mood for small talk and could barely be civil. She listened for several minutes as he spoke. Julia could hear his voice, pleasant and concerned. Alexandra continued, "I have so much on my mind right now that I can't make any decisions about anything. If you say I have to come down, I'll come down. Shall we leave it at that?"

She paused while listening, the expression set on her face. He must have asked what it was she had on her mind, but in the next instant, she went on a tirade like Julia had never heard come from her.

"Things like taking seven little kids to a child psychologist, getting them their first immunizations they have ever had so they can get into school for the first time in their lives, buying a three-bedroom apartment for three million dollars, and going back to my job to pay for it." She listened more.

"I don't think that is a good idea. Why? For one thing, I don't have time for it. What would be the point? Well, if you have to personally interview them, then so be it." She listened for a while longer, then put the phone down without saying goodbye.

"What was that all about?" Julia asked, flabbergasted. What more was going to happen here?

"He wants to come up here to talk to the kids! It's the last thing I'm prepared to deal with, if you want the truth. But it's better than hauling them down there." Alexandra was thinking about how it was starting to get dark out already and she hadn't even picked up the babies once today. It made her sick. She wasn't going to let time be the enemy in her life. She needed to get those doctor appointments made before another day passed.

She picked up the phone again and called her office. She apologized to May, telling her that it could wait until the morning, but she needed appointments for the children with a child psychologist, dentist and pediatrician. May already had the latter taken care of thanks to Peter Van Sant.

"The head of pediatrics at the hospital will see all the kids tomorrow morning at ten. Bring the forms you need signed, and all will be well." May went on to tell Alexandra some nice anecdotes about her patients, who missed her, and how the OR was ready to kill Eb and only tolerated him because his partner was so wonderful.

Her positive and validative conversation uplifted Alexandra. But she wasn't in the mood for small talk and was barely able to say, "Thank you."

May didn't expect any response, and as soon as they hung up, immediately picked up the phone again and called Grace, giving her the lowdown on the conversation.

Alexandra picked up the first baby she came to after hanging up the phone. It was Moira. Alexandra thought Moira looked a lot like Elizabeth when she was a baby. Spidery limbs, red hair, huge eyes, she giggled, like an orangutan baby. She responded to her grandmother with smiles and cooing, grabbing her finger and trying to shove it in her mouth. Lowering herself into a rocking chair, Alexandra sadly thought of the day, coming up this week, when she would return to work and leave the babies with Beth. Suddenly, she thought it was time for a talk with Beth, who had come when it was an emergency and saved the day, with Faye's help. Alexandra hadn't given any thought if she was suitable or not. It was the path of least resistance. As soon as she could, she would take Beth aside and talk to her about what her vision for the children was and what her beliefs were regarding child rearing. Better late than never.

Alexandra gently placed a sleeping Moira into her crib and picked up Morgan, who was chewing on a squeaky toy. "A goo goo, Momma," she said. Alexandra patty-caked with her and held her by her waist so she could stand up on Alexandra's legs. She loved the sensation of standing.

"It won't be long before she's walking," Beth said. Alexandra hoped she would be home the day Morgan took her first step.

∂∽◌

She initiated her new schedule on the second day with the children. Picking up each baby, sitting each little child on her lap for a story or a talk, this would be her daily routine from now on. She would have to fit in time with the children on workdays, but since the only hobby she had was running, she thought it would be easy. She was misinformed, but would grow used to the amount of work, as all parents did.

Beth announced that it was time for dinner, and she would fix soup and sandwiches. Alexandra reminded her that they lived in Manhattan, and she could order and have delivered anything her heart desired. Beth was happy to do the cooking until Maria started working the next day. When they finished eating, Alexandra told them it was bath time and time to get ready for bed, generating lots of moans. Then she pointed out that since there was only one bathroom in the apartment, getting ready for bed would take a long, long time, so bedtime was still several hours away. She told Beth to take a break; she'd manage bath time if Beth would listen for the babies. She'd sent Julia back to the hotel in a taxi, protesting all of the way. But she could see that sleeping in the hotel would be preferable to sleeping with Alexandra, who snored.

Beth dug a paperback out of her bags and put her feet up to read. Alexandra helped the children find their pajamas and underwear in their individual containers. She ran the bathwater in the tub. She filled the bathroom sink up with water. Morgan loved getting naked, flipping over on her stomach as Alexandra tried to take off her diaper. She also loved the sink bath, splashing and screaming with glee. She tried to get her to lay still to dry her off, but Morgan was too fast. She crawled naked as fast as she could out of the bathroom, out into the living area. The other children screamed with laughter. Alexandra finally got her corralled and two of the older children into the tub. Nina and Gloria were encouraged to have privacy. It felt good to Alexandra to get all seven children bathed and changed into clean pajamas. It was important to her, for whatever reason, that they be clean upon going to bed. She remembered that it was just a few weeks ago that she had to be reminded to bathe.

By nine thirty, all was quiet. She gave her bed over to Beth, who seemed truly grateful. Beth hadn't stopped for three days and deserved a decent sleep. Alexandra could sleep anywhere, and being out on the sofa was better. She wouldn't be listening to the breathing of the babies all night and could get up and go out early for a run.

At ten thirty, her cell phone beeped the characteristic beep of a text message. It was Detective Ryan. He would take an early flight out and arrive in Manhattan by ten. He'd call her to set up a time that would be convenient to see the children. She had to take the children to the hospital for the pediatric visit, so he would have to wait. She messaged him back that information, and he replied that it was fine. She didn't want to deal with him, because she was afraid of him. He seemed interested in her romantically. She was aloof, but not dead. She was aware of the attraction between certain men and herself. But there was no interest whatsoever for her.

She also wasn't interested in women, so it wasn't a sexual preference. During college, she realized that she didn't need a social life. The things her peers did, the places they went didn't interest her at all. During her first year of medical school, she gave in to a persistent young man who would not stop pursuing her. He was quiet and studious, athletic and determined. He asked her out continuously for six months, and she finally gave in, thinking that perhaps some feeling, or sense she was missing something, would appear if she played the role properly.

They studied together, went for runs around the city, had a slice of pizza and a beer, and then finally, slept together. She was disappointed because it meant nothing to her. The act itself was perverse. When he climbed on top of her, she felt like she was having a medical procedure. Weirdly enough, her body responded appropriately. But she knew that just meant she wasn't dead. When he finished, she waited as long as she could stand it, slid out of bed, dressed, and got out. She avoided him, didn't return his calls, and he finally gave up.

Back in Chelsea, the next morning before sun up, she slipped her running clothes on and tiptoed out of the apartment. She stayed out for two hours, thoroughly revived and rejuvenated. It was freezing cold; the air was crisp and pungent with smells of the river. Only other very early rising runners were out. She remembered her promise to acknowledge the owner of the coffee shop, so when she went in for her morning cup, the first thing she did was tell him how much she appreciated his store.

"Oh!" he said, shocked. "Well, thank you for coming in. Coffee's on the house today."

Alexandra smiled, but left her bills on the counter and got out before he could protest. Also on the streets, bread trucks were delivering to the restaurants, and the smell of fresh bread made her hungry. The bakery on the corner was open, and she walked in and got a dozen hot bagels. When she let herself in the apartment, the family was starting to stir. When they saw her, the little ones ran to her and hugged her legs. Beth was feeding Moira and had Nina giving Morgan a bottle. Alexandra relieved Beth so she could take the bagels into the kitchenette and start breakfast.

"Thank you for feeding Morgan," Alexandra said to Nina. Morgan was struggling to sit up. "You can probably try giving her the bottle to hold." Nina let the bottle drop, and Morgan picked it right up, and they laughed.

Marie arrived and jumped right in, taking over in the kitchen so Beth could relieve Alexandra, who had to get seven kids to the pediatrician by ten. How was this going to work? How did poor people do it? How could she have gone through the past years and still be so unenlightened?

Selfish, self-centered, self-absorbed. Those were words that she'd use to describe her lifestyle. Slowly, she would change it. She would give of herself, find ways to repay those who served her over the years, like Julia. Julia practically raised her, gave selflessly, dropped her life at the slightest need and ran to help Alexandra. She had to be repaid somehow, in time given back or something monetary. Maybe they'd go on a vacation to a tropical island after Christmas. As she got into the shower, she imagined taking her family to Disney World or on a cruise. She held her face up to the warm water, and for the very first time in a long, long time, she enjoyed the feel of the water flowing over her.

She'd be devoted to the children who only had her in their life. She'd give them all of the love that she wanted to give to their mother. For twenty-seven years, she'd suffered, waking up every night sick to her stomach with a tearstained face, angered, longing for a tiny baby that she'd held for a few brief weeks when she was only a child. There was a new life now awaiting her. She would have to reinvent herself, unsure how to find the way, but knowing it would come about in steps. Her family was waiting, so she didn't linger for much longer, turning the water off and reaching for a towel. From then on, her shower would be something enjoyable.

They made it to the hospital in time for the appointment. Her colleagues came to the Pediatric Department to meet the children; May, Grace and Virginia and several of the other nurses from the OR, even Peter Van Sant. Seeing everyone gave her the desire to get back to work. It would be good for her to start delegating at home and get her routine adjusted.

Chapter 23

While the children thrived with the attention they were getting in New York City, in a different part of the country, their mother was on the road to health. Almost a week had passed since her last dose of illegal drug. Along with sobriety came a resurgence of genius; she was her mother's daughter and, unfortunately, her grandmother's. She was angry that they'd put her in jail and livid that the woman who said she was her birth mother was responsible for putting her there.

She'd already worked her manipulative magic on the seasoned therapists. One, a woman nearing retirement, agreed that it was criminal she'd lost custody so quickly, her children given to someone no one knew of and who didn't even come from the area. A perfunctory background check was done on Alexandra, covering her medical license and her address, but that was all. They'd taken her word that she was Colleen's mother. The therapist arranged for an attorney friend of hers to see Colleen. He was young and altruistic. He believed the underclasses got a raw deal in the criminal justice system. He felt Colleen had a case against the state.

Although Colleen did have a prior record, nothing in her file suggested she was an unfit mother. The police documented squalid living conditions, but giving the parent a warning to clean it up was how they normally handled it. The older children weren't going to school, but the mother claimed to be homeschooling. Emergency Room records substantiated a short narrative that the oldest girl had given regarding a sexual abuse allegation. It wasn't clear who had taken the child to the hospital the first time; the usual paperwork with parental signatures to allow treatment was missing. That in itself wasn't grounds for custody transferal, however. The mother didn't rape the child. It was never clear who had, although it was allegedly someone the mother knew.

There was talk in the neighborhood that the mother had had a baby two years earlier that no one ever saw. There was speculation that she killed the newborn, but no proof and no investigation. Then he made an appointment to meet with Colleen. She had a lawyer on the books, but all she had to do was fire him. He wanted to do a little poking around before he saw her on Friday.

About the same time the lawyer was reviewing records for Colleen Rodríguez, Tom Ryan was in a taxicab in Manhattan, going to meet with Alexandra and her grandchildren. He had already checked in with the police department in the city, as was the usual procedure. When Alexandra called him yesterday with the latest news, he knew that it was just troubles on the surface, much more might be lingering below. He felt an urgency that he couldn't explain. Something else was brewing; he heard from another detective that the mother had a new lawyer who was an ACLU pain. She was chomping at the bit to get out of jail and get her children back. Tom wanted to keep her incarcerated for as long as he could so he had the time to gather as many facts as possible.

Alexandra was becoming a real distraction for him. He was trying to help her, yet the very thought of her was a stumbling block. Physically, she was so appealing, tall, lanky, and lean. Calling her odd was an understatement. But she was so dry, and he was attracted to that. Tom also had the reputation of being an oddball at work. *Maybe they were kindred spirits.*

The taxi pulled up to her building. It was not what he expected. It was a newer building than those found in the Quarter, and ugly. He would find out soon how much of it was hers. She told him yesterday that she was buying the unit above hers for three million dollars. He was curious to see what three million bought in Manhattan. He paid the driver and got out of the cab. He could see lots of people through the glass in the front door. As he went up the steps, he saw it was children and a couple of adults juggling strollers and babies, filling the lobby. Then the door opened.

Alexandra saw him at once and was unexplainably annoyed. *I'd better pull it together,* she thought. She forced a huge smile on her face, splitting her lip in the process. Julia and Beth said hello to him, smiling and excited. Beth was playing the coquette, holding her stomach in and batting her eyelashes. The little performance was so obvious, but rather than being embarrassed or irritated, Alexandra was grateful. Any attention Beth could give him would be less that Alexandra had to.

They were walking to school to return the filled out forms and show the girls where they would be spending their days. The energy was palpable. Alexandra gave Tom a choice to wait or walk along with them, and he, of course, took the latter. Alexandra had Gloria's and Sophia's hands, and she held on tightly. Tom walked along with them, heading up the group. Alexandra focused on the girls, asking leading questions to help them express what they were feeling as they walked the short distance to school.

They loved it. Gloria asked, "Is this my school?" Ben struggled to get out of the Hitch Hiker and was yelling, "School, school, I want to go to school!"

Tom made a mental note of the kids' exuberance. It might be important if the custody issue went back to court. He was glad for this small outing with the kids. Hopefully, it would help them relax when he had to ask them the really tough questions.

When they got home, the babies went down for a nap. Alexandra lay down with Ben to tell him a story, hoping he would sleep for a little while. She didn't have to be there during the interview, and she didn't want to hear what they said. She agreed that if the children requested her to be there, she would. A social worker from the Department of Child and Family Services in New York came, and they taped the interview, as well. Julia and Beth both were interviewed.

"Alexandra, Alexandra," Julia said, stroking her forehead and whispering her name. Dube was sitting in a leather club chair, naked. Her mother was there, dressed in an evening gown, smoking a cigarette, calling her name. She woke from a dream.

"What?" She opened her eyes.

"We're done. You should come out." She left and went out of the room.

Alexandra swung her legs over the side of the bed. She sat on the edge for a minute, thinking. She went into the bathroom and looked in the mirror. She looked like hell. She took a slug of mouthwash and spit it out into the sink. When she walked out of the bedroom, Tom was standing by the kitchenette, drinking a glass of water. He watched her walking toward him. The admiration in his eyes made her self-conscious. She felt like a robot, legs and arms walking stiffly in unison. He looked at *her* like she was on a runway. It infuriated her, making her stiff walking worse. She squelched the urge to tell him to get out. He was there to help.

"Do you want to go for coffee? I'd like to talk to you."

She paused for a moment and could think of no good reason not to. It would be of benefit to the children.

"Okay," she said, resigned. "I could use a cup."

She went into the children's bedroom and spoke to Julia and Beth. Maria was going shopping for school uniforms with Loren, taking the three older girls along. Alexandra knew how fortunate she was; she didn't have to lift a finger and the work was done. They told her to go with the detective; they would be fine.

She grabbed a coat and nodded at Tom. He followed her out of the apartment and down the stairs.

"Where's your new space?" He'd forgotten to ask earlier.

She pointed up the staircase and turned around to go back up. "Follow me. I haven't even seen it since I bought it."

He followed her silently. When they got to the top of the staircase, she reached around the top of the door and found an old-fashioned skeleton key, fitting it in the keyhole. She opened the door and walked in, Tom following. They entered a light-filled space, high ceilings with moldings around the perimeter. It had two and a half bathrooms and three bedrooms and a den. They would use the kitchen in this space as the family kitchen. The den would become a room for Beth, if she stayed. The lower apartment would continue to be Alexandra's bedroom and office. She spoke in a monotone, reciting facts, pointing out the few details of the apartment she knew as though he were the buyer, not she. He was impressed with the home the children would have after the way they'd lived in the Ninth Ward.

Finally, she had enough. "Let's get out of here. I want that coffee."

They strolled across Twenty-Third side by side, not talking.

"I don't know what to say to you," she said.

"You don't have to say anything," Tom replied.

"I should thank you for trying to protect my grandchildren," Alexandra said. She was struggling to find that balance; he was a good man who'd flown all the way to New York to make it easier on her grandchildren, yet she was feeling hostile and angry with him.

"Look, I'm just doing my job," Tom replied. "You've had a load of troubles dumped in your lap, and boy, you really can handle yourself. You're an impressive lady."

Alexandra wanted to throw up. She started walking faster, and he lengthened his stride to keep up.

"Here it is," she said, as they approached the coffee shop. "Let me get it." Coffee was a lot more expensive in Manhattan than New Orleans.

"Eight bucks for two cups of java? Jesus Christ. Oh, excuse me," he said. "If you get this, I take you to dinner tonight."

"Get the coffee, then," she said, stepping back and gesturing with her hands.

He looked at her and gave a hearty laugh. She was tough.

She waited while he paid for the coffee. They walked back out of the shop and sat on a bench on the sidewalk, across the street from her apartment. The coffee was good. Just what she needed.

"Do you want to talk at all about what I'm here for?" he asked.

As annoyed as she was with his visit, she thought it was considerate of him to try to keep her informed.

"Not really. Yes," she replied. "Although I don't want any gory details, if that's okay."

He told her the cleaned-up version of the interview he did with her grandchildren.

"But that's not the only reason," he added. "There's talk in the station that your daughter has a new lawyer, one who is working the angle that she was wrongly incarcerated and the custody ruling in your favor was inaccurate. The rape allegations don't involve the mother unless we can prove that it occurred in the house while she was there and it was her friend who did it, with her knowledge. But that was before the latest allegations." He paused and looked at her, concerned. "Do you want me to go on?" he asked.

She nodded her head.

"I want to get back to New Orleans as soon as possible. If what the children are saying is true, there may be videotapes in your daughter's house. We never went into her bedroom when we got the children the other night. I can get a search warrant based on these allegations, and search it tonight." He took a sip of coffee.

Alexandra's anxiety level was rising as a new concern surfaced. Why didn't he arrange to have someone looking for the tapes when they'd called him that morning? He was wasting valuable time.

"Are you saying I could lose the children?" she asked.

He looked at her and nodded. A new wave of fear swept through her. She just couldn't lose them now. Life would not be worth living if she did. It would just be awful, so empty and meaningless. In three days, she felt like she'd been given a second chance for happiness. Maybe it was premature to have placed so much hope in seven little children. But the judge had said "permanent custody."

"She didn't seem to have an interest in the children. What would make her want them now?" she asked.

"I have a hunch that it is purely monetary: sales from the videos, their welfare money, and also, prostitution when they get older. It's all conjecture, but I can prove it if those videos exist." He was getting fidgety, looking up a telephone number on his blackberry.

"I'll get my reservation now." He spoke to the airlines and was able to get a flight out at six. He would be there for a few more hours. She didn't know what to do with him. They sat and drank coffee. He was pensive, looking at his watch, occasionally writing down notes.

"Let me try another tactic…" He pushed a button, must have been speed dial, and keyed in some words and put his phone back in his pocket. Several minutes later, it beeped. He pulled it out again and read. "Okay, I got an earlier flight. Sometimes it pays to be a cop." He stood up and offered his hand. For a split second, she was going to ignore it, but took it instead. He let go the moment she stood. "I'll call you tonight if I'm able to resolve anything, okay?"

She nodded yes. Suddenly fickle, she wanted him to call her for more than news about videos. She stifled the feelings. No more complications. It was obvious she didn't know what she wanted. They crossed the street in silence, walking the few steps to her apartment.

He followed her up the steps and into the vestibule of her building. Before she could open the door to the hallway, he gently put his hands on her shoulders to turn her around. She resisted and considered pushing him away from her, but gave in. He'd taken her by surprise. He pulled her closer, wrapping his arms around her.

"I'm so sorry you're going through this," he said softly. He stroked her head.

It felt good to her, friendly and nonsexual. She was in a sort of stupor, not knowing what to do, never having been held like this before, not even when she was a child, in memory. She was afraid that if she pushed him away, she'd fall to the floor. Not trusting her legs to hold her up, or her mouth to speak words he could understand, she allowed the intrusion. Allowed it and slowly, without thought, began to accept that she needed it. She needed another human being to support her, physically and emotionally. She'd barely talked since he arrived. But if he thought well of her, more power to him. She didn't need to control things, never had. She was more than willing to allow others to be in charge. He wasn't hurting anything by holding her, and it felt good. She fell into him, her body relaxing. When the time was right, she stepped back, Tom still holding on to her shoulders. He didn't try to kiss her, didn't expect anything in return. She was slightly smiling, with a dreamy, half-closed look to her eyes.

"I better get back to the airport. If anything happens tonight, you'll be the first to know, okay?" he said.

"Sounds good," she said. "Thank you for coming all this way for my grandchildren." She took a step back and turned to open the hallway door, not really wanting to see him go, but feeling awkward in his presence now. "Good-bye, then. Call me." That was all she could give him.

"Okay, I will," he said. He opened the door and walked out.

She peered out the sidelights and watched as he walked down Twenty-Third, turning to see if a cab was behind him, and when one drove by, he flagged it down. She didn't go up until she saw the cab disappear down Eighth.

Her family was occupied in the apartment when she walked in. Marie was in the kitchenette, preparing a simple dinner. It was a calming, lovely scene, unusual in that there were seven children and four adults in a space of about six hundred square feet, and it felt like a fine fit. They said hello to Alexandra. Julia asked if Tom was coming up, and she explained that he was on his way back to New Orleans to do some investigation. Nina looked up at her grandmother and then back down at the book. Alexandra couldn't be sure if she was worried about exposing the horrors of that house or grateful for being rescued. She chose not to worry about it right now. She would do what was necessary to protect the children, and that was that.

Tomorrow the children would start school. The three older girls would spend the day with a series of tutors. The little ones would go to a nursery school. Julia was returning to New Orleans. Alexandra knew it was time for Julia to get back to her life, but it made her sad to think of her going away. She'd enjoyed having her around.

Alexandra was returning to work, too. She would spend the day reviewing charts, and then she would meet those patients on the operating table soon. May confided that the OR was having a welcome-back luncheon for her. They hated her partner, hoping he would go away for a long, long time.

"Eb has a generous heart," Alexandra said, loyalty for him strong.

"Well, I'll quote you," May replied, laughing. "He's been in a pretty decent mood this week, now that he knows you're coming back. Peter Van Sant was in here this morning, begging me to call you and ask you to come in. Eb heard him and came out swinging. 'Get the hell out of here! Don't you have anyone else to pester?' They yelled at each other for a few minutes, and then Peter said, 'Call her, call her. I demand that you call her!' It was a zoo. Of course, all the patients in the office heard them. It's amazing he hasn't alienated the whole city." It sounded like she was getting back just in time.

❧❧

After dinner, Alexandra repeated the routine of the night before. She managed to shave a half an hour off bath time because she gave the girls more independence. She felt pride that her grandchildren would be nicely dressed and never have to worry about classmates teasing them about smelling or having bad breath. She imagined what Christmas would be like in a few weeks; tomorrow she'd involve her staff in plans for a lavish Christmas. Just a few days ago, Christmas would have come and gone without a nod. Her accountant had reassured her that there was enough money for her family to live a very different lifestyle than she'd lived. Her grandchildren would have the best of everything.

At ten that night, children in bed, Moira up and fussing but Alexandra enjoying her company, her phone beeped. It was Detective Ryan. He was in court, waiting for the emergency judge to rule on his search warrant. The bad news was that Colleen's new lawyer was making some headway. There was a letter waiting for Jeff Gauguin, a summons really, which outlined the new custody hearing.

"What does this mean? Is she going to be released? Are the children going to have to go back to New Orleans?" Alexandra felt increasing fear. She just couldn't lose them.

"I'm not sure where it will lead. She might be released. I can't imagine the judge reversing his original ruling. It would be a first if he did. Do you have a lawyer?" She did here in New York, but no one down there. *Oh God, she wished she could take the children and hide.*

"I can get a lawyer, but do you really think I'll have to defend myself? I never asked for the children in the first place. They were awarded to me by the system," she replied.

"You can't be too safe, Alexandra. Look, I have to hang up. The judge just arrived. Will you be up later?"

She told him she would be, to please call her as soon as he heard anything.

She put her feet up on the coffee table. Coffee table? Loren must have brought it in today. It was handy, already covered with children's books. The fireplace had a fire in it, soft light filling the room. Moira was riding an invisible bike, reeling arms and legs. She wasn't going to go to sleep anytime soon. Alexandra bent her head down and blew tiny raspberries on the baby belly. She would happily sit holding her all night. She never needed much sleep anyway, had probably gotten more in the past five days than usual. The phone beeped again.

"I've got the warrant," Tom said. "I'm going back to the house tonight with two other officers. Why don't you get some sleep, and I'll call you in the morning?"

"Call me before seven if you can; I'm going back to work tomorrow." She didn't know what more to say. Except, *get over to the goddamned house.*

The next morning at five, Alexandra was running down Avenue D. She couldn't sleep for most of the night and knew she would be a mad woman all day if she didn't get at least an hour in. It would calm her, help her stay focused. The old doubts were creeping in. The old desires to shut down, fog over, were struggling to surface. Somehow, for the sake of her grandchildren, she had to remain in control. She had to be normal.

Julia was going back to New Orleans. They'd said their goodbyes last night. She wanted to be there as Alexandra's proxy. When she got back, Beth was managing alone with Maria. Loren would be in to help any minute. Alexandra took a quick shower and put clean running clothes on; she would run to work now that there was no one telling her she couldn't. Beth looked at her with a combination of admiration and jealousy: that body. Not an ounce of excess flesh. Beth planned to ask her if she could join in as soon as they hired another person to help with the kids. As Alexandra was tying up her shoes, Nina came out, dressed in her new clothes.

"Oh, my goodness, look at you!" She put her arms around the little girl, who hugged her back.

"Are you going to work? Why are you dressed that way?" Nina was confused by the wet hair, no makeup and spandex.

"I get to dress this way because I run to work, and then I change into surgical scrubs." She straightened up. James would take her briefcase and a change of clothes to the hospital. She made sure she had her phone on her, but everything else went into the case.

"Okay, I'm off. I'll miss all of you today! But I have to make some money so we can keep up this fancy lifestyle." She surprised herself at her sudden wit. She left the apartment and ran to work. Just as she was walking into the main entrance, her phone beeped. It was Tom.

"Well, someone was here earlier. The place was ransacked. All it means is that we can't prove without the children's statements that there was videotaping of sex acts involving children. It means that she may get out of jail sooner than we hoped. That's all it means." He sounded like he was trying to convince himself, and she told him as much.

"We will just wait and see," he answered. "Let her attorney make the first move. I have another angle I'm looking at, something I don't want to repeat on the phone or without some proof. Keep your fingers crossed."

They said good-bye, and she walked in the building. A group of doctors and nurses ran up to her, patting her back, shaking her hand. She had a smile plastered on her face and felt like a robot.

Peter Van Sant came out of his office to her rescue, announcing loudly, "Doctor Donicka! How wonderful to have you back! Come into my office, please," and pushed her toward the door to his suite.

"Jesus Christ, Sandra, hold all my calls, will you?" he said to the receptionist. "Come on, Alex, have a seat. Tell me what has been going on the past couple of days."

She gave him the scoop on the kids, Loren's cousin, how things were falling into place. She left out the gory details, the sex tapes, the possible custody battle looming.

"I need to get back to the OR, Peter. It will help me stay on an even keel. These past days, I almost felt normal. I've had conversations with people. I, what's the word, *related* to people. I felt like I wanted people around me." She was looking down at her hands, beautiful hands with long, tapered fingers. Surgeon's hands.

"My dear, no one here knows better than I that you are a normal, hard-working, gifted, brilliant person! Should anyone suggest differently, there'll be hell to pay." He sat next to her, reaching for her hands.

She looked at him. "I hope you're right, Peter. I hope I am normal."

They stood up together, his arm around her shoulders. He could feel the bones under her sweatshirt. There had to be a way he could protect her.

She threw herself into the day. There was a pile of charts in the office. Each came with MRI films, EEG results, everything she would need to make a diagnosis. Her partner came in at lunchtime. He'd treated her with respect, giving her a chance when she was so young to be an attending surgeon at the highly regarded institution, offering her a partnership as soon as she finished her residency. He'd paved the way for her success so she could keep her grandchildren, the transformed, adult Elizabeth already forgotten.

"Come to lunch with me, Alex," he said.

She didn't argue, and they walked side by side to the cafeteria. They discussed all of her upcoming cases. He would make sure she would be able to pay for her fancy new apartment. He was concerned for her and offered all the help she would need. She took so little from their practice; maybe it was time it gave to its most valuable member.

At two that afternoon, Tom called her. Colleen was out of jail. She was out, and she was pissed. The courts ruled in Alexandra's favor that morning. Alexandra thanked him and ended the call. She needed to get back to work. Worrying about Colleen wasn't going to help anyone.

She was finished with the charts. May was calling patients who had all of their preadmission testing done to come in Monday morning for their surgery. It would be a full day. She was almost a week behind with her cases, mostly complex craniotomies. All of the patients would be admitted the morning of surgery. Eb had taken care of the surgeries that were in-house: emergency AVMs, a few brain tumors that were causing pressure to build in the skull, serious problems that couldn't wait for her. He knew she was a better surgeon than he was, and it was good for business that she liked the OR, he the office. They complemented each other. He would do whatever it took to protect her. *Even if it means lying and cheating,* he thought with a chuckle. Not that it should ever come to that.

She was walking to her private office to change out of her work clothes and put her running gear back on when her phone beeped again. She heard the voice, felt a chill go up her spine.

"I'm coming to get my kids. You didn't really think it would be that easy to get them, did you, Mother?" Colleen said softly.

"I didn't come to take your family, Colleen. The court gave them to me to care for until you were well enough to provide for them." Alexandra was trembling and trying to keep the nervousness out of her voice. "Everything I said to you, I meant."

"That's bullshit!" she screamed. "Give me your address. I'm coming to get them as soon as I can. I'll take a bus all night if I have to. And don't tell anyone I'm coming, I mean it."

"Where are you calling from?" Alexandra asked.

"What difference does it make?" she answered. "I'm at a friend's house. But I'll be leaving for the station soon."

"Colleen, why not stay here in New York with me? Let me take care of you and your children. I have enough for us to have a wonderful life. You'll never want for anything, I promise you." Alexandra knew it sounded like she was bragging again, but she didn't care.

"I have plans for my kids, and they don't include you. I'm going to have my own bunny ranch, right here in New Orleans. I don't need you or your goddamned money. But I need my girls." Her voice was proud, triumphant.

"What about Ben, Colleen? What good will he do? What good will a boy do? Leave him with me at least," she said, pleading.

"Ben's lucky he's alive. I had another boy right after he was born that I killed with my own hands. And you're lucky you're alive. I should have killed you the day you came to my house. If you try anything, I can kill you. I have a gun."

The conversation confirmed what Alexandra feared, that her daughter was insane, if she needed anymore proof. If Colleen did have a gun, it should have surfaced when the house was searched. She thought of the inept police work, the videotapes missed the first time they'd gone into the house, and how none of this would be happening if they'd searched it then.

"Call me when you get here, Colleen. I'll meet you at the bus station and bring you to my home. When do you think you'll arrive?" She was playing her daughter's game now. "I know the kids will be thrilled to see you. They miss you so much. It's been really hard these past five days." She kept up with the lies, soothing her daughter's fractured spirit.

Colleen was tough, though. She manipulated but thought she was immune to it.

"You're damn right I'll call you. I'm leaving now."

Alexandra hung up the phone and left the hospital. She gave her briefcase to James and asked him to take it home; she'd get home on her own.

Chapter 24

On the day of Colleen's phone call Alexandra decided she'd run for a while before heading directly home. Her mind was swirling as she walked away from James and the limo and waited on the corner for the light to change. The tone of voice Colleen used was so familiar. It was her dead mother, Catherine's voice. Alexandra remembered with clarity the day she'd run to The Black Swan after discovering the baby was gone. Confronting Catherine, who then threatened to kill the baby. Now Colleen would come to New York and get her children, all seven of them, if it meant killing her or killing them. Alexandra felt her mouth stretching into a hideous grimace as the thoughts piled up, but she stopped and admonished herself. There would be no de-escalation into madness. As soon as the light turned green, she took off in a sprint.

Running was the religious vehicle that could take her to a higher place. Its gentle repetition cut through the chaff of senseless worries and confusion, providing a medium for thought, for decision-making. She calmed down; her resolve to keep her grandchildren safe strengthened. No one would ever do that to her again, take someone she loved away from her, no matter who she was.

∂∽∾

It was dark out and lightly snowing when she got home. The children were wired, Beth said, crazy to talk to Alexandra while they waited for her. They were crowded around, hugging her legs, grabbing her hands, trying to drag her to the table so they could tell her about their day. Maria took Alexandra's fleece hat and mittens to hang up as she allowed herself to be dragged.

"One person at a time, children!" she begged. "Let's start with poor Ben. He always goes last."

"I went to school today! I drawed. I learned my name. B-E-N-J-A-M-I-N. I can write it, too!" he said.

"Very good, Ben!" they chorused. Maria picked him up and sat down with him in her ample lap.

"Taylor's next," Nina said.

"I went to *nurthrey* school," she said. "I wrote my name, too." She proceeded to spell Taylor. Everyone clapped. She grinned from ear to ear.

"Kindygardeners are five years old," Sophia said. "I can spell my name, AND I can spell Granny's name, and the name of our street!"

"My clath ith right acroth from Thophia'th clath," Gloria said, lisping through the gaps in her teeth, an ear-to-ear grin. "My teacher'th name is Mith Thmith."

Alexandra started clapping to cover up the laughter building in her chest and the giggling starting among the other children. Gloria was so proud of herself. Her teeth couldn't come in fast enough. She was anxious to tell more, but Nina spoke up first.

"I love my teacher. She wore a pretty outfit. She also smells good. I want to go back tomorrow." She looked at Alexandra. "Can I go back?"

"Of course! This is what little girls and boys do. They get up each morning and go to school to learn lots of interesting facts so they can go to college someday."

"Did *you* go to college?" Gloria asked.

"She's a doctor, silly!" Nina answered.

Yes, I went to college," Alexandra said.

"Your momma must be rich," Nina replied.

"No, my mother was very poor. I went to college and medical school on scholarships Julia helped me get," she explained, deciding that sounded better than telling them about threatening Dube. "When I was in school, I got good grades, and when it was time for me to go to college, the colleges came looking for me. All of you can have that same experience, if you study hard and do well in school." It was more words than they had heard her speak at one time. Then she thought, *Julia! Oh my God,* she'd never called her. Colleen's call, momentarily forgotten thanks to the children, came back to her with a hot flash that made the bile in her stomach come into her mouth. She excused herself for a moment and went into her room. She brushed her teeth and drank some water.

Julia picked up on the first ring. She wouldn't listen to any apologies. "Don't be silly! You worked all day and came home to a houseful. How'd the first day back in the mines go?"

Alexandra gave her the short version of the day, emphasizing the positive highlights and the excitement of the children after their day in school. They talked for ten minutes. Alexandra missed her good friend. She would have never gotten the family to where they were now if it weren't for Julia. She never mentioned the call from Colleen or the news from Tom.

After they hung up, she got ready for bed. It would be good for the others to see her in her pajamas, in for the night. She fully intended on going for another run later, but it would be well after the children were tucked in and everyone else was asleep.

Maria made a pot of chamomile tea and fixed a plate of cookies for their bedtime snack. "I love being here so much, miss, I wish I could stay all evening to help you and Beth with the children."

Alexandra smiled and patted her arm. Maria had heard from Loren that the doctor was cold and uncommunicative, and Maria didn't get that from her at all. Loren was pleased when she'd described this other face of Alexandra.

"Maybe you bring out the best in her," Loren said. "Definitely the children do."

"She sure loves those kids," Maria said. "I've seen a lot of mothers, and she loves them like they are her own kids. I can't imagine having seven of them pushed on me and handling it as well as she is."

"Boy, if you knew her like I do, you'd be even more shocked," Loren said and then, whispering, added, "She could barely dress herself a week ago. We had to remind her to bathe, Maria. It was bad." She made a gesture of waving while holding her nose.

"No way! Well, you'd never know it now," Maria said.

"Yeah, something definitely has changed for the better, like she's had a healing or something. It's a real miracle," Loren said.

Now, as Maria drank tea with Alexandra, she was baffled at Loren's description. This woman sitting across from her was one of the kindest she knew.

Chapter 25

Alexandra lay on the couch in the dark. She was listening to the silence of the apartment. One of the older children was snoring. She'd given Moira a bottle at one, so she'd sleep through until five.

At two thirty, she got up and pulled her running clothes back on, tucked her cell phone in her jacket pocket and zipped it shut. She arranged the pillows on the couch so it looked like she was still sleeping there just in case Beth got up; she didn't want her to worry. She tiptoed to the front door and carefully opened it so as not to disturb anyone. Beth slept like a dead person, but she didn't want to alarm Nina. She quietly let herself out of the building and walked down to the corner, turning north on Eighth. Once she was off her street, she started to run, flying over the miles, aware of the night, of the people still out on the street. She never felt safer. As if in a dream, her feet barely touched the ground. She ran farther and farther north, Eighth turning into Broadway, a neighborhood in which she felt she could be herself. There was no pretext.

At three, her phone rang. It was Colleen, calling from a phone on the street. She was clearly frightened. "Come and get me, will you? There are creeps *all over* this place."

Alexandra told her she would be there soon. She turned around and ran south again, toward Forty-Second Street. Port Authority was safe enough; there were usually police all over the place. Alexandra asked her to wait where she was, a phone booth outside of the Majestic Theatre. She was there in twenty minutes. Colleen looked at her like she had two heads.

"Are you robbing banks? What's with the getup?" she said sarcastically.

"It's what I wear to run in," Alexandra explained. "Let's go somewhere and have a cup of coffee, shall we?"

"I don't want any fucking coffee," she said loudly. "I've been on a bus for twelve hours. I want my kids." She was angry, unreasonable.

Alexandra felt she had to get her to talk. She had to allow her to be in the children's life. If she had never met them, it would be different. Now, life would be insurmountable without them.

"Take me to my kids. I broke parole coming here. If anyone finds out, I'm dead. I gotta get those kids and get back on the bus and be home by tomorrow afternoon. You can give me the money for airfare. If you love them so damn much." She made a face at Alexandra.

"Okay, I could do that. It would be easier for you to fly home," she answered, remembering the chaos of flying with seven kids, even with three adults. Alexandra looked over at Colleen. There was no way she would be able to walk twenty blocks to the apartment. "Let's take the subway down to my place."

Colleen was looking around at the area, trying to hide her excitement at being in New York.

They walked back to the Port Authority. At this hour, there wasn't anyone around, not even police. *They must be fighting crime somewhere else tonight.* They walked down the stairs of the empty station together, shoulders almost touching.

Perhaps if life had been gentler, the ravages of drugs and abuse erased with a magic wand, the women could have passed for twins they were so alike. Alexandra sensed something profound was about to take place within her, freeing her from the constrictions life had placed on her. All the years of heartache, emotions frozen, pointless days—the crushing disappointment that occurred when she'd finally reached her life's goal culminated in this moment.

She could hear the express train approaching the station, distant screeching of metal on metal, and she inched closer to the edge of the platform, willing her daughter to follow her example. Stretching her body as safely as she could, she strained to look into the black tunnel as though there were important things to see. Elizabeth wanted to see, too, and stretched her body over the edge. When the train shot into the station, it frightened her. All Alexandra had to do was stick out her beautiful right hand and, with her finger, poke Elizabeth in the ribs. With the gentlest push she flew off the platform into the path of the train, almost into its side, it was so close.

The train was well into the dark tunnel before the confused conductor figured out what had happened, while the slender feet of a runner, quick and sure, struck the pavement above.

<<<<>>>>

Also by Suzanne Jenkins

Pam of Babylon is the first installment of the *Pam of Babylon* series. Although it may be read as a stand-alone novel, character development is on the continuum of all five books in the series. The following are the *Pam of Babylon* series, available on Kindle and in paperback on Amazon.com. Follow the links to Amazon.

#1 *Pam of Babylon* Long Island housewife Pam Smith is called to the hospital after her husband Jack suffers a heart attack on the train from Manhattan. It is the beginning of a journey of self-discovery and sadness, growth and regrets, as she realizes a wife and mother's worst nightmare.

#2 *Don't You Forget About Me* The family begins to sift through the evidence of a life of deceit, putting together the pieces left behind by Jack.

#3 *Dream Lover* A gritty, realistic portrait of the aftermath of deceit, more pieces of the puzzle come together as the women each attempt to go on living in the wake of despair. More characters are introduced, including Ashton.

#4 *Prayers for the Dying* Jack Smith's victims attempt to move forward while grappling with the pain and horror that he left behind. Pam makes startling revelations about herself, while Sandra hopes for a future with exciting expectations. Marie is in a most unlikely place, with the happiest news in the bleakest circumstances. Ashton's story of a lifetime love affair with Jack is finally told, with his heartache revealed.

#5 *Family Dynamics* Heartbreak and devastation move toward triumph in the fifth and final installation of the *Pam of Babylon* series. Pam is at last able to overcome the pain of Jack's rejection and her own role in perpetuating his deviance, when she meets Dan and falls in love. Her children move on with their lives in ways Pam would have never believed. Sandra fulfills her dreams with Tom, and a gift from Marie helps to complete their life together. Ashton and Ted build a beautiful life, and new discoveries make it richer than they thought possible, but with a twist. But don't be deceived; what you hope for is not what you may get.

⇛⇝

The Greeks of Beaubien Street is the first book in The Greektown Trilogy. Although it may be read as a stand-alone novel, character development is on the continuum of all the books in the series.

Nestled below the skyline of Detroit you'll find Greektown, a few short blocks of colorful bliss, warm people and Greek food. In spite of growing up immersed in the safety of her family and their rich culture, Jill Zannos doesn't fit in. A Detroit homicide detective, she manages to keep one foot planted firmly in the traditions started by her grandparents, while the other navigates the most devastated neighborhoods in the city she can't help but love. She is a no nonsense workaholic with no girlfriends, an odd boyfriend who refuses to grow up, and an uncanny intuition, inherited from her mystic grandmother that acts as her secret weapon to crime solving success. Her story winds around tales of her family and their secret laden history, while she investigates the most despicable murder of her career.

The Greeks of Beaubien Street is a modern tale of a family grounded in old world, sometimes archaic, tradition as they seek acceptance in American society. They could be any nationality, but they are Greek.

The Princess of Greektown is the second book in **The Greektown Trilogy**. Thirty years ago, Terry Smith was Detroit's top news anchor. She set the standard for excellence in investigative journalism, staying at the news desk long after her time should have been over. Just as Terry's son-in-law is murdered in the city, Detective Jill Zannos faces upheaval in her own life. A new man, family intrigue and the dregs of the last case she investigated becomes the lowest priority as she and her partner Albert untangle the mess of Terry Smith and her family.

రిపొ

Alice's Summertime Adventure

We meet Alice Bradshaw when she is at a crossroad. She's just beaten cancer and is suddenly unsure of what her next move should be. Looking back on where she's been and what the future may hold, she knows she needs to make a big change in her life. Then her car dies on the highway after an argument with her daughter. Dave, a stranger on a motorcycle, pulls alongside her and saves the day. He offers Alice a chance at adventure. She jumps on it, much to the dismay of her children. The adventure starts a chain of events that will have Alice and her children, as well as Dave, questioning every aspect of their lives. There will be a few casualties along the way, a lot of anger, life changes and a few shocking surprises. *Alice's Summertime Adventure* is the story of an average American family as they struggle with dilemmas we all have, and making choices that aren't for everyone.

Atlas of Women A Collection of Short Stories

Women are the heart of the home. (Unless it's a home with a man as the heart!) This volume is about women. The stories are a melding of truth from my own experiences and fiction created from both observation and fantasy.

Mademoiselle, a novella, started out as young adult genre. But as I wrote, Philipa grew up into a young woman who found her way after a short detour, choosing the more difficult path.

The Golden Boy ended up exactly as I imagined it would. A family deals with a loved one's mental illness with love and support, but when there is no longer any hope for normalcy, prayer and grace allow them to step aside.

Tribute to a Dead Friend is my tribute to every woman who's lost a close friend but continues to be inspired and comforted by her spirit.

A Night Encounter, currently published on Amazon, is a short story about regrets and self-forgiveness. A daughter's disrespect borne of sibling rivalry comes back to haunt her in a most unusual and gentle way. As in every work, there are elements of truth in the story, but it is pure fiction. I spent time in my garden last summer, convinced my late mother was there with me. It was a very therapeutic and comforting experience.

Vapors, selected to appear in Willow Review 2013, is a fantasy in which a wife discovers a way to make her presence known after her husband reveals a painful secret.

For preview and purchase information

visit: http://suzannejenkins.net